Beyond the Picket Fence

and other
short stories

LORI WICK

SweetRiver Press
Eugene, Oregon 97402

Verses marked NASB are taken from the New American Standard Bible, © 1960, 1962, 1963, 1968, 1971, 1972, 1973, 1975, 1977 by the Lockman Foundation. Used by permission.

Cover by Terry Dugan Design, Minneapolis, Minnesota

Beyond the Picket Fence
Copyright © 1998 Lori Wick
Published by SweetRiver Press
Eugene, Oregon 97402

Library of Congress Cataloging-in-Publication Data

Wick, Lori.
    Beyond the picket fence / Lori Wick.
        p.   cm.
    Contents: The camping trip—Christmas for two—The haircut—Beyond the picket fence—An intense man—Be careful with my heart—The Christmas gift—The rancher's lady.
    ISBN-13: 978-1-59681-007-5
    ISBN-10: 1-59681-007-6
    Product # 6810075
    I. Title
PS3573.I237B48   1998
813'.54—dc21   97-31382
                                                                          CIP

Printed in the United States of America.

        06 07 08 09 10 11 12 / BC / 10 9 8 7 6 5 4 3 2

Contents

Books by Lori Wick

A Place Called Home Series
A Place Called Home
A Song for Silas
The Long Road Home
A Gathering of Memories

The Californians
Whatever Tomorrow Brings
As Time Goes By
Sean Donovan
Donovan's Daughter

Kensington Chronicles
The Hawk and the Jewel
Wings of the Morning
Who Brings Forth the Wind
The Knight and the Dove

Rocky Mountain Memories
Where the Wild Rose Blooms
Whispers of Moonlight
To Know Her by Name
Promise Me Tomorrow

The Yellow Rose Trilogy
Every Little Thing About You
A Texas Sky
City Girl

English Garden Series
The Proposal
The Rescue
The Visitor
The Pursuit

The Tucker Mills Trilogy
Moonlight on the Millpond
Just Above a Whisper
Leave a Candle Burning

Other Fiction
Sophie's Heart
Pretense
The Princess
Bamboo & Lace
Every Storm

This special book,
my first book of short stories,
is for my mother,
Pearl Hayes.
Thank you for the example you are
to me. Thank you for trusting God
even when you can't see tomorrow.
I love you.

Acknowledgments

A step away from the norm is so fun. I like routine and even like some of the ruts I'm in, but a time-out from the everyday action is great. This book provided that for me, and these are the people I'd like to thank for taking that break with me.

My first note of thanks on this book of short stories is for Carolyn McCready and LaRae Weikert of Harvest House Publishers. In that meeting in Denver, you liked the idea the moment you heard it. And also for Julie Castle, who wasn't in the first meeting, but whose enthusiasm when she heard of this book was just as great. Indeed, she started thinking up cover ideas within moments. Thank you, dear friends, for all the support and encouragement.

I also wish to mention Eileen Mason. You were the one who took a chance and recommended publication of my first book. If it weren't for your vision, Eileen, I would never have developed a readership, and this book would never have worked. Thank you.

Thank you, Roxie Carley, for your listening ear. You have heard these stories and ideas for dozens more, and yet you never tire. You always listen with patience and enthusiasm, and laugh in all the right places. You're so special to me.

Thank you to my sweet husband, Bob. Thank you for liking my ideas and for trying so hard to make everything in the manuscript look good. I would be lost without your guidance, not just on the computer, but in life. I'm so thankful that we're not a short story. I hope our book will read on for at least 70 years.

Dear Reader

Welcome to my world. *Beyond the Picket Fence* is a small look into the way I exercise my imagination. I might need a break from the book I'm working on, or I just might be between big projects, but when those times come, I work on short stories.

These stories are sprinkled all through my computer in various stages. Some are still at the title stage and others need only a memorable ending. The eight stories in this book are the only ones I've finished. I hope you'll be blessed as you read about special characters that have come to my mind, but whose stories were not long enough to become a full-blown manuscript.

I didn't try to work with a theme or put the stories in any particular order, but I had fun and I hope you will too. I also added small notes about what each story meant to me. I hope these will be special to you as well.

Maybe this book will be just what you need—light, easy to read, something to relax with. Or maybe you'll be challenged in a way that only you and the Lord could know about. In every case, I pray that God will bless you as you read.

Warmly in Christ,

Lori

Be Careful with My Heart

Sing for joy in the LORD, O you righteous ones; praise is becoming to the upright. Give thanks to the LORD with the lyre; sing praises to Him with a harp of ten strings. Sing to Him a new song; play skillfully with a shout of joy.
Psalm 33:1-3

❧ ❧ ❧

Casey Sheridan rubbed her damp palms down the front of her slacks as the plane taxied to the gate. The ride had been bumpy, but her case of nerves had nothing to do with the ride or landing. However, it felt good to disembark, and Casey walked into the terminal with a determined stride.

Her hesitancy returned when she was met by a sea of unfamiliar faces. She had no idea who was supposed to meet her and wished all of a sudden she had asked about that.

The group began to clear, and still Casey stood alone. She had checked her one piece of luggage and wondered if she should go and collect the bag or stay where she was. As it was she had no time to decide; a familiar face was headed toward her at a breakneck speed.

"Dan!" Casey's voice showed her relief, and she was grabbed in a bear hug that nearly lifted her off the floor. "What are you doing here? I was sure you'd be with Janelle."

"She refused to leave unless I stayed to see you safely to the church. I only just put her on the plane a few hours ago." His voice was breathless as he spoke, and he was obviously very excited. "Come here and sit down; I'll tell you everything."

Making themselves as comfortable as the airport seating would allow, Dan began. "First of all, what did Janelle tell you on the phone?"

"She said she was pregnant and that the doctor ordered complete bed rest. She had to quit the tour, and would I come and fill in for the last six weeks. Are you sure she's all right? I couldn't tell on the phone if she was telling me everything."

"She wasn't telling all," Dan said with a shake of his head. "A week ago she fainted, and we blamed it on fatigue from our rough tour schedule, but when she fainted again, I rushed her to the hospital. A pregnancy test came out positive, and after the doctor got her dates, he decided she is about three weeks along. She's also severely anemic.

"The doctor kept her in the hospital a few days, and that gave her mom time to get down here. Like I said, they only got away a few hours ago. I'm booked on a flight that leaves tonight after I see you out to the tour."

They sat in silence for a moment before Casey spoke. "Janelle told me she had given up on ever getting pregnant. Now that she actually is, does the doctor think she'll go full term?"

"It's too soon to tell, but the bed rest will help, and she's not spotting or feeling any pain." Dan stopped for a minute and looked intently at Casey. "We want this baby, Casey; we want him so much. I think for the first time I have an inkling of what you have been through."

Casey reached for Dan's hand and squeezed it gently. "I'll pray, Dan. Whatever God has for you will be perfect. Right now you might believe you can't be happy without that baby, but our God is wholly sovereign. Ask Him to help you see that His will is perfect."

The next half hour was spent in retrieving Casey's luggage and then getting to the car. Once on the road, Dan gave Casey a light sketch of what her job was to be.

It started out sounding relatively simple. Janelle played piano for her brothers, the Riley Brothers, a trio specializing in contemporary Christian music, presently touring the southern part of the United States. They had been on the road since May and were near the end of the tour now.

Of the six weeks left in the tour, the first two would be spent doing nightly concerts, for which Casey would be playing the piano in Janelle's stead. The following three weeks would be spent at a summer Bible camp in the mountains. The last week was reserved for a few days of vacation and getting the bus home to northern California.

Casey was needed to play for the group during the evening meetings at camp but would have her weekends free. Janelle and the three men of the Riley trio were also scheduled to be camp counselors. Again, Casey would be expected to take Janelle's place. Casey had listened in silence up to this point, but her eyes widened at this bit of news. She turned her head and stared at Dan in something akin to panic.

"Now, don't get excited, Casey," he reassured her when he glanced over and saw her look. "You'll do just fine. The first week is fifth- and sixth-grade girls, the second is seventh and eighth, and the final week is high school, freshman and up. I think you'll love it."

Casey continued to stare wordlessly at him until he began to squirm. "Well, I mean, I hope you'll like it. You get along well with everyone, and I'm sure the girls will look to you for spiritual guidance, and, you know, look up to you as a woman." Dan stumbled to a halt as Casey continued to stare at him.

"Why do I get the feeling I'm in for six weeks I will never forget? If I hadn't seen the sincerity in your face, I would say Janelle staged this whole thing to get me out more."

Casey was again staring at the man behind the wheel, but Dan was saved from replying as he pulled off the freeway and into busy downtown traffic. Within minutes he was parking the car in a large church parking lot. A huge silver touring bus was parked across many spaces, and Casey felt nervous at having to meet all the people that bus would surely hold.

She began to muse, not for the first time, at how strange it was that even though the Riley family had been to visit Janelle, Casey had never met them. She and Janelle lived in the same town and were close friends, but each time the Rileys were in town, Casey had been away.

Casey and Janelle's mutual love for music caused them to hit it off on their first meeting. It wasn't long before Casey was sharing with Janelle things that she shared with few people. Janelle's husband, Dan Green, turned out to be as precious as his dear wife, and the three of them enjoyed each other's company immensely.

"Who is taking your job as manager, Dan?" Casey asked as they crossed the lot toward the building.

"Brad." Brad was the oldest of the trio, and Casey knew him only by name. "His wife, Chris, is along, and between the two of them, they'll manage with only two more weeks of actual road tour."

The inside of the church was cool and spacious, and as they walked through the foyer, Casey's head turned in all directions, taking in the visitor's table, bulletin board, and other things familiar to most church lobbies. Before she knew it, they were at the sanctuary doors. Casey wasn't sure she was ready but followed Dan inside.

The introductions were awkward, and the musically talented family she was meeting was little help. Brad and Chris came forward and shook her hand, and Casey appreciated the gesture even if their smiles were a bit sad, but Casey met Hunter from his place at the piano. He stood but did not come forward to shake her hand. Morgan, the youngest member of the group, was even less cordial. He did not stand or move out of his seat but nodded slightly as they were introduced.

Casey's mind scrambled around for everything Janelle had ever told her about her brothers. She knew that Brad and Chris had children but that Hunter was a widower. Morgan was not married, but she thought he might be engaged.

Casey's mind was still moving when Stan, Brice, Rich, and Terry were also introduced. Casey was to learn later that they were in charge of the bus as well as all sound and operating equipment.

Walking Dan back out to his car, Casey felt like a child being left alone for her first day of kindergarten. She tried to hide her misgivings behind a bright smile, but he was not fooled.

"Listen, Casey, most people think the people in Christian singing groups are all saints. But in truth these men are hurting right now. It doesn't really have anything to do with you; it's just that they've never toured without Janelle, and they don't think anyone can play like she can." Dan chuckled before he continued. "They didn't believe her when she said you played better than she did."

"She told them that?" Casey nearly groaned.

It was Dan's turn to stare. He shook his head slowly as he spoke. "You really don't realize the depth of your musical ability, do you? I love my wife, and I think she plays beautifully, but Casey, I've never heard *anyone* play a piano like you do."

Casey could only stare at him before looking away in confusion. Playing the piano was no effort for her, and she was more than a little guilty of taking her talent for granted.

"You'd better go, Dan," Casey said, breaking the silence. "Please give Janelle my love and tell her I'll do my best."

Thinking about the people inside, Casey stood for a time after Dan drove away. *Please, Lord, comfort them at this time. Help them to accept Your will in this. Please give me the right attitude and words if needed. And most of all, Lord, help me to glorify You with this talent I take for granted.*

🌹 🌹 🌹

"What did you think of her?" The question came from Brad as he faced his brothers, his wife, Chris, by his side.

"It's not whether or not we like her, Brad; it's just hard to go on without Janelle. And we really don't know if she can play. I feel a little funny about that," Morgan said quietly, and for a time everyone was silent.

Hunter broke into the quiet. "I'm sure Jan would never send us anyone who couldn't do the job, but like Morgan said, it seems strange not to have Jan here. Dan said he'd call as soon as he got home, but I'd give anything to be there myself."

Conversation came to an awkward halt as the group watched Casey come back into the room. She was completely unaware that the uncertainty she was feeling was clearly written on her face.

❧ ❧ ❧

Sixty minutes later Casey had changed into a comfortable pair of baggy shorts and a cotton top. She'd noticed on the first introduction that everyone was dressed casually, and with the temperature in the 90's, Casey welcomed the change.

At Chris' suggestion, Casey had stowed her belongings in the bus. Chris had been wonderful, showing her around the bus and talking to her like an old friend. The men had some errands to run, so the two women had lunched together in the bus. Most of the conversation during the meal was taken up with talk about Chris and Brad's two girls. They hadn't seen them in weeks and couldn't wait to arrive at camp where they planned to meet.

"My parents are bringing them up," Chris explained. "We talk on the phone every few days, but it's not the same."

"Tell me how old they are again." Casey asked with genuine interest.

"Kim is 13, and Linda is 10."

"And they're with their grandparents?"

"Right. My folks come and live at our house when we tour, so the kids have the security of being home. I flew home almost a month ago to see them, but we won't be with them again until they come to camp." Chris' eyes were suspiciously wet, and Casey smiled in understanding.

From that point the conversation moved to topics far and wide, and Casey found herself relieved that Chris had not pressed her to share about her own family. The men arrived back just 20 minutes later, and it was time for Casey's first practice session.

❧ ❧ ❧

"Janelle told me that you're familiar with our music," Brad said to Casey from his place across the piano.

"Dan gave me a portfolio of everything," she told him as she took a seat before the keys. "I've looked over anything that was new to me."

"Great. Let's start with *Over Yonder*."

Morgan and Hunter straightened from where they had been relaxing against the piano and moved into position on either side of Brad.

Casey did not need the music for that piece, and with casual ease she played the rather lengthy intro-duction. Just several notes after the introduction, however, she stopped. The men had not joined her on their note, and since all three faces, sporting expres-sions she couldn't interpret, were turned to her, she assumed she'd made a mistake.

"Too slow?" Casey guessed.

"No," Hunter said softly after a moment. "It wasn't too slow. Please play it again, and this time we'll come in."

Casey's fingers went back to the keys, and just as Hunter said, their voices rang out clear and pure. It was a beautiful number, and Casey loved being this close to them as they sang. She'd heard their records and tapes but never heard them live. She found herself swept away by the blend of praise to God in perfect harmony.

Speaking the first spontaneous words since she arrived, she exclaimed, "That was wonderful," a huge smile lighting her face.

"Yes, it was," Morgan agreed, finally smiling. "Janelle told us you played well, but we had no idea."

"That wasn't what I meant—" Casey began, only to be cut off by Hunter.

"I don't suppose it was, but Morgan is right. Play something else, Casey." Hunter's smooth bass voice made her feel as if something had just rocketed up her spine. Casey's eyes went to the keys, confusion filling her as she pondered her reaction to Hunter. She could feel her face warming slightly, but the men must not have noticed; when she played *Sweet By and By* they joined in with the ease of breathing. From there they moved to two other songs that were new to her, but Casey never missed a beat.

Seeing that Casey would need no further work, Brad cut the practice session in half, telling her that she was free until warmup in a few hours. As she rose from the piano bench, Chris approached and handed her a schedule for the next two weeks.

She took a moment to look it over and would have asked questions, but Chris obviously had other things on her mind, since she darted off without another word. Standing near Casey, Hunter watched her but did not speak. Casey didn't think she should direct any of her questions to him, so she felt more uncomfortable than ever.

She glanced at him and then back at her schedule before casting her eyes over the auditorium that held more than 3000 seats. As she looked out over the floor and balcony, Hunter's presence was forgotten.

Those seats would be full of Riley Brothers fans tonight, and she, Casey Sheridan, music teacher at Thompson Jr. High School, would have to play the piano as they listened.

"Don't think about it." Hunter's voice came softly to her ears, and Casey started. She could only stare at him.

"You won't be able to see past the first rows, at least not for the first few numbers. By the time the house lights go up, you'll know you're going to be fine."

"How can you be so sure?" Casey asked as she pushed one damp palm into the pocket of her shorts.

Hunter's brows rose as though he found Casey's question insulting. "I've just heard you play" was all he said before moving on his way.

🥀 🥀 🥀

The evening's performance was upon Casey before she had time to be nervous. With only one mistake and one surprise, it was a wonderful night, one that Casey would never forget.

The men had all been ready to launch into *Sweet Jesus,* but Casey had played "Homeward Bound." The audience was ignorant of any error, but after the number, Casey saw on her music schedule that she'd blundered.

The surprise that came a few numbers later was of a different nature. While still backstage, Brad had told her to keep playing no matter what. Casey thought this a bit risky but did as she was asked. She learned the reason when she started *At the Feet of Jesus*. The men never came in. She soloed the entire piece, the trio turning on the stage to watch her. She received a wonderful ovation for her effort.

The men had been quite pleased with themselves, and the entire crew had all shared a good laugh while having coffee in the bus later that night. Casey fell into bed sometime after midnight, her heart ready to praise God for this special day, but she fell asleep before she could shape any of her thoughts.

$$\text{❧ ❧ ❧}$$

Big Pines Christian Campground was one of the most beautiful places Casey had ever seen. The ground was a carpet of pine needles, and the air was so clean and crisp that she could have stood in one spot for an hour, simply drinking in the beauty and fragrance. Everyone in the group, all longtime visitors to this camp, enjoyed her reaction. Well, almost everyone. Hunter was still keeping his distance.

For two weeks now they'd lived and worked in close proximity, and Casey had grown close to everyone but Hunter. While never unkind, he was neither warm nor approachable. The others had talked of their families, their hopes, dreams, and prayer requests, but Hunter usually remained silent.

Casey knew he wasn't quiet with everyone. She had noticed that when it was just family, he laughed and talked comfortably with Brad, Chris, and Morgan. When the group met, however, even if Casey was the only nonfamily member, he said little if anything.

He did, however, do much observing. Casey had grown proficient at not paying him excessive attention, quite an accomplishment since she was becoming very aware of him. Maybe this was the reason she would often glance up and find him studying her.

She never let her eyes linger on his, but she asked herself repeatedly why he didn't approach her if he found her so interesting. Casey did a mental shrug. She was honest enough to admit to herself that she would have welcomed a little attention from Hunter, but she figured it wasn't part of the Lord's plan or it would have happened already.

"Casey," Morgan broke into her musings. "If you'll gather your gear, I'll show you to your cabin."

"Oh, sure. Is it far?"

"Not bad. Your cabin is tucked back into the trees, but it's close to the women's shower room. Your seven fifth graders do not arrive until Sunday, so take advantage of the peace and quiet."

"I have all fifth graders—no one older?"

Morgan smiled at her disbelieving tone. "It won't be so bad. At least you're not getting what I'm getting."

"What's that?"

"Fifth-grade *boys.*"

Casey laughed at the look of mock horror on his face and went into the bus to retrieve her things.

❧ ❧ ❧

A heartfelt sigh escaped Casey when she woke from her nap. She had used the dresser next to the one double bed in the cabin to put away her things and then spread out the sleeping bag Morgan had said was hers for the next three weeks. When she was finished, the bed looked so inviting that Casey stretched out and fell almost immediately to sleep. Now she was awake enough to see the dial on her watch and was surprised to see that she'd slept for more than two hours.

Casey swung her feet to the floor with two purposes in mind—heading into the small bathroom in the cabin and then eating. Lunch had been so long ago that she felt hollow inside.

Fifteen minutes later she walked through the trees, her nose leading her in the direction of food. Someone was cooking over a grill, and Casey found herself praying it would be the Rileys. She felt it would be most unfair to smell something this wonderful and not get a taste of it.

"We wondered when you would join us," Morgan called to her as soon as she came into view.

The entire group was there plus a few people Casey didn't know. She walked with unconscious grace, her long legs encased in blue jeans and a white cotton blouse tucked in at the waist. The wind teased her shoulder-length blonde hair around her lovely, tanned face.

"Casey," Brad began, "come and meet the camp directors, Marcus and Lizzy Peterson."

"It's good to meet you, Casey," Lizzy offered with a smile after they'd shaken hands.

"Your camp is wonderful."

"We rather like it," Marcus told her with a grin. "How is your cabin?"

"Just great."

They talked for several more moments, both of the Petersons working to make her feel very welcome. She was told that the other counselors, as well as the guest speaker, would be coming the next day, and that the campers would arrive on Sunday sometime after lunch.

Casey was then introduced to Kim and Linda Riley, who had finally arrived with their grandparents. After she met the girls, Chris teased her.

"We'd begun to think we'd lost you," she commented with a smile, referring to Casey's nap.

"No," Morgan put in, a teasing light in his eye. "Hunt checked on you and said you were snoring to beat the band. I'm surprised we didn't hear you all the way down here."

Casey smiled but didn't say anything. She sincerely doubted that Hunter had been anywhere near her cabin, but the thought of his hearing her snore was humiliating. Thankfully, dinner was proclaimed ready, and Casey was able to hide her embarrassment when she chose a plate and got into line.

❧ ❧ ❧

"You don't snore."

The words came so softly to Casey more than two hours later that she thought she'd imagined them. They were, however, all too real. Casey turned from where she had just thrown away her paper plate and cup to find Hunter standing behind her.

"What did you say?"

"I said you don't snore. You looked upset when Morgan teased you, so I thought I'd reassure you." His deep voice was serious but kind.

Casey blinked at him. "You actually came and checked on me in my cabin?"

"Uhm hm. We were supposed to have a meeting at three o'clock, and everyone wondered if you were all right."

Casey's hand came to her mouth. "I forgot all about that meeting."

"Come on, everyone!" Brad, still standing over by the fire pit, called to the assembly at large. "We're ready to light this fire and get down to some serious campfire activities."

Hunter moved off without another word to Casey. She followed behind him feeling vaguely irritated, at whom she wasn't sure, but she was angry. He'd come to reassure her, and all he did was make her feel foolish. It had been a long time since Casey had felt any real interest in a man, and when she finally did, he had to be one who was horribly aloof and still wore a wedding ring years after his wife had died.

She was so angry right then that she wondered what she had ever seen in the man. Oh, he was tall and good-looking, and he sang like an angel, but beyond that, she decided he wasn't worth her time. Her anger began to work like a purge as she walked. Casey suddenly didn't care if Hunter looked at her or completely ignored her. In a way she felt something of a relief settle over her, but she also knew this wasn't a right attitude.

As she sat on a log that helped make up a ring around the fire, Casey did some serious praying. If this campfire was like others she'd been a part of, there would be singing and sharing. She couldn't do either in the mood she was in now. By the time Brad finished telling everyone what a great job they'd done on tour and how much he was looking forward to these weeks at camp, Casey had taken care of things. Just in time too, since Kim said she wanted to sing.

❧ ❧ ❧

Two hours later the sky was very dark, and the temperature was dropping. They had sung every song they could think of, but now everyone had gone for jackets before meeting back at the fire to make s'mores. Casey was just finishing her second one when the sharing began.

Marcus Peterson shared some riotous stories from the family camps earlier that summer, and then Hunter related something someone at their last concert had told him when they were signing albums and tapes. When he finished his story, a comfortable silence fell on the group. After several moments Brad's voice broke the quiet, taking Casey completely by surprise.

"I know I didn't ask you about this earlier, Casey, but I wondered if you might share your testimony with us."

Casey did not immediately reply.

"I know you feel put on the spot," he went on, "but we've come to love you in these weeks, and hearing how you came to Christ would be really special."

Casey smiled across the fire at him and Chris, who sat beside him. Chris' parents had taken the girls off to bed, but she could feel everyone else's eyes on her face.

"It's a rather long story."

"We've got time," several people chorused. So with that Casey began.

"I grew up as an only child in Bakersfield, California, but in the middle of my junior year of high school, we moved north to Sacramento. I wasn't raised in a Christian home, and I remember giving my parents a pretty hard time about the move. However, it wasn't as hard at the new school as I thought it would be. I made friends very quickly and even tried out for the varsity cheerleading team for my senior year.

"Well, I made the cheering squad, and during that year I got close to a boy named Nathan." Casey's voice had grown very soft, but she was looking at the fire and didn't notice the intense attention of her audience.

"He was captain of the football team, and I was head of the cheerleading squad. We were homecoming king and queen, and it seemed like the perfect match. However, Nathan was a believer and I was not. His family strongly disapproved, but he rebelled and saw me anyway. They were never hateful to me, but I was a real concern to them. We started dating before Christmas, and I'm sorry to say that by the time we graduated, I was two months pregnant."

Casey had come to realize now that every eye around the campfire was glued to her, but she continued gently.

"We really did love each other, so we married just a week after school was out. My parents had no problem with it at all. In fact, my father set us up in a small house, one that had been my grandmother's. I had been unhappy at home for a long time, so I was just glad to escape. It wasn't much fun for Nathan. He began to grow weary of a sick, crabby wife and the weight of responsibility. He didn't leave me or even lash out at me. He did something in my opinion that was far worse: He went back to church.

"At first I was so hurt I didn't know what to think. Then I got angry. Life was pretty miserable for a time, but Nate stuck with me. Although I was still bitter that Nathan believed he needed others besides me, after our daughter, Alison, was born, I simply poured my life into her.

"When I think back on it, I don't know how Nathan stood it, but he kept working at the marriage, and I finally began to come around. I was not comfortable discussing church or the Bible with him, but when he attended, I no longer became angry. He used to take Alison, and I would feel very alone on those Sunday mornings. Still, my heart was hard toward God."

Casey paused now, and although she didn't seem to be fighting for control, she did stare intently into the fire before continuing.

"Alison was 14 months old when our house caught fire one night. We had no smoke alarms, and since Nathan and I were both sound asleep, the house was filled with smoke by the time we woke up. The house was quite small, so Nathan nearly dragged me from the bedroom and pushed me down the stairs toward the front door before running for Alison's room. Neither of them ever made it outside. They both died of smoke inhalation."

Here again, Casey took a deep breath. She could hear someone crying, but she didn't dare look beyond the fire, or she would never finish.

"It was a horrible night, as you can imagine. The families gathered on the lawn, and I eventually went home to my parents' house and finally fell into an exhausted sleep about midmorning the next day. When I awoke sometime after two o'clock, Nathan's brother, Neil, was sitting next to my bed.

"I didn't know it at the time, but Neil had been praying fervently for my salvation. He told me that lately he'd been begging God to save me, no matter what it took. He said, 'I've lost my brother and my niece, but I know where they are. All I care about right now is you, Casey —you and your lost eternity.'

"My heart broke on those words, and I knew for the first time that I was as lost as he'd said. Neil brought out his Bible and read to me how much I needed a Savior, how Jesus Christ was willing to be my Lord. I won't tell you that I never looked back, because I did, but God has never left my side.

"I think I'd better end by telling you that I'm all right," Casey said with a small smile as she took in the swimming eyes all around her. "I went back to school and now have a bachelor's degree in education. I've been teaching music at a junior high school for two years. In and of itself, time is a healer, but with Christ the changes are forever. It's been over nine years since Nathan and Alison died, and as much as I miss them, I honestly don't believe I would change a day."

No one spoke. Never dreaming of the depth of her pain or God's provision, Brad had innocently asked Casey to share. One by one the group stood and came to her. Casey stood also. The family and crew, most of them with tears in their eyes, hugged her and thanked

her for sharing. The last one to stand before her was
Hunter. He didn't hug her but looked at her for the
space of several seconds.

"When you're ready to turn in, I'll walk you back to
your cabin."

"All right," Casey said after just a moment.

"Thanks, Casey." It was Brad again. When he'd
hugged her earlier, words had failed him; now he came
back to speak with her. "That couldn't have been easy
for you—thank you."

"You're welcome, Brad. It is a hard story, but I think
it's good for me to talk about it from time to time."

Overcome with her sincerity, Brad hugged her
again. "Chris and I are turning in now. Breakfast is just
a walk-through between 8:30 and 9:00. I'll see you
then."

"Goodnight," Casey told him and everyone else as
they began to disperse. She turned toward her cabin,
Hunter falling into step beside her. A flashlight suddenly flicked on from his hand and they walked quietly
up the hill to Casey's cabin.

Casey had not thought to leave any lights on, so she
was glad for Hunter's flashlight. He opened her door
for her and flicked on both the inside and outside light.
Casey stood looking at him under the yellow bulb, not
saying anything but trying to search her heart where
this man was concerned.

Having put both lights on, Hunter was ready to
turn and speak to Casey. "Did Jan ever mention to you
that I'd lost my wife a few years ago?"

"Yes, I knew you were a widower," Casey said softly.

"I have a tendency to think that no one has ever experienced the depth of pain I have, or that anyone could possibly understand what I'm going through," Hunter admitted. "When you shared tonight, it was a good reminder to me that we all hurt. My wife has been dead for over two years, and I still feel married. I still feel unfaithful if I'm attracted to a woman. You made yourself vulnerable before all of us tonight so we could see how God works. Thank you, Casey."

With that he wrapped his arms around her. Casey's eyes slid shut for the brief moment she returned his embrace. She felt more confused than ever. Was he trying to tell her that he did care for her? Casey simply didn't know. She had told herself not to give him another thought, but if he opened his arms once again, Casey knew she would be strongly tempted to walk right back into them.

"That's an interesting look I'm getting," Hunter commented, and Casey started. She hadn't been aware of her expression.

"I'm just trying to figure you out, Hunter Riley." Casey returned, opting for total honesty.

"Am I such a puzzle?"

"Well, now, you tell me. I come into this group, and you're all a little standoffish at first. Understandable, considering the way Janelle had to leave, but the others have all warmed up. You seem to keep some sort of guard up between us, but at the same time you watch me intently." Casey's voice held no rebuke; in fact, she still had a few more gentle words.

"Now you come to me in all sincerity and tell me you still feel married. Am I supposed to believe that you would be interested if you could get beyond your wife's death?"

It wasn't a question that needed an answer, and Casey could see Hunter knew that.

"I see what you mean," he told her after just a moment's thought.

"Please don't misunderstand me, Hunter. I really appreciate your honesty, and I'm sure you realize I'm not demanding answers, but I'd be made of stone if I didn't wonder where I fit in, or if I fit in at all."

Hunter nodded, a curious light in his eyes. "I'm glad you're ready to wait for answers, since I don't have any right now. I'm also glad you told me how you feel."

"What exactly did I tell you, Hunter?" Casey wondered if they really understood each other.

Hunter tipped his head to the side in a way that Casey found adorable. "I think you said that if I asked you on a date, you'd go."

Casey smiled. This was the most bizarre conversation she'd ever had.

"I'd better go in and let you be on your way," Casey said after a moment's quiet, thinking she was more tired than she realized.

"Was I right?" Hunter asked, not ready to drop the subject.

"I don't know." Again Casey was very honest.

"In other words, I'd have to ask you to find out."

"No, Hunter. My words were not intended as some sort of challenge to you."

He tipped his head again, and Casey turned her head away. She was certain he had no idea what he did to her heart.

"Goodnight, Casey," he finally said when Casey didn't look back at him.

"Goodnight, Hunter," she echoed and moved inside. She waited until she heard his footsteps moving away from the cabin before turning off the outside light, locking the door, and getting ready for bed.

❧ ❧ ❧

Since Casey had enjoyed a nap, it would have been understandable had she been the one to lie awake, but this was not the case. Casey slept almost immediately. On the other hand, Hunter lay in the dark of his cabin for hours.

His first wife had been a wonderful person. Gail had been warm and giving, dedicated to Christ and Hunter. But two years was a long time, two and a half to be exact, and Hunter wondered why he still felt so odd when he thought of marrying again.

Maybe it was because he'd never met a woman like Casey Sheridan, one who had endured such pain but still chose to serve God. She was warm and fun and so pretty that Hunter just wanted to stare at her. She was also so gifted at the piano that Hunter could have listened to her play for hours. So why was he holding back?

Morgan thought Hunter was just out of practice and told him so, but when Hunter tried going without his wedding ring, even for a few hours, his hand felt naked.

"Maybe I need to give it more time," he said softly to himself in the dark. "I'd like to move on. I'd like to love again; I just don't know if I can. If I had been the one to die, I would have wanted Gail to find someone new to share her life."

Hunter stopped speaking out loud but continued to bare his heart to the Lord. He asked God to help him move wisely where Casey was concerned, but at the same time he wondered why he didn't just go ahead and let his guard down with her. He already knew that she was a wonderful person, and without ever having really experienced it, he somehow knew that she would always deal with him compassionately.

Hunter would not have been quite so content with his plan if he'd understood how vulnerable Casey was to his status as a widower or the sensitive way he walked her to the cabin and stayed outside to talk.

☙ ☙ ☙

"Okay now," Marcus spoke into the small public address system as the kids were finishing up with breakfast. The fifth- and sixth-grade campers were having the time of their lives, and it took a moment to get their attention.

"This being the last day of camp, I told you we would have some special surprises. If you think the Rileys have performed for you on these other evenings, wait until you hear their last concert tonight."

Marcus was given no chance to go on, since the room erupted with cheers. He spoke again as they quieted.

"But we've got a lot of great things to do before then. Right now it's time for the staff hunt." Again the room shook with cheers. "As you finish with breakfast, the counselors will hide. Finding them means points for your team.

"Don't forget now, some will be in pairs and worth extra points, and of course, the team that finds our speaker, Pastor Chris Bauer, gets 1000 points." Marcus continued to speak, even though mayhem met this announcement. "Go ahead now, staff, and head outside. Hide well. You know the places that are off limits."

Casey said goodbye to her adorable crew of girls— one or two even needed to hug her—and made for the door. Brad was there holding it for her, and Morgan was waiting directly outside. She was paired with him for extra points.

"You're going to hide with Hunt instead of me," he informed her the minute he saw her.

"I am? Why the change?" Casey didn't mind; in fact she was pleased, but Morgan had an odd look on his face.

"I'm always paired off, and I want to hide alone."

Casey's look was clearly skeptical.

"Go on now," Morgan commanded, lowering his voice since Hunter was just coming from the dining hall.

"Okay," Hunter said as he stopped beside Casey, his eyes on a small square of paper in his hand. "I guess you and I are together."

Casey glanced down at the slip and noticed that the handwriting was different from the original paper she'd seen, the one telling her she was paired with Morgan.

Casey sent a glance toward the youngest Riley, but he only grinned at her. Obviously finding himself very clever, he ran down the steps of the dining room deck.

Casey was tempted to shake her head. Between Morgan and Hunter, she felt as though she'd been going in circles all week.

"We'd better get started," Hunter broke into her thoughts, and Casey followed him down the steps.

"So where do you think?" he asked.

"The archery range?" Casey suggested.

"No. Brad and Chris always hide there."

"In back of the kitchen?"

"No."

"We could climb a tree."

"Last time I did that I got sap all over my pants."

Casey came to a stop on the trail.

"What's the matter?" Hunter looked at her in surprise.

"You must have someplace in mind, Hunter, since all of my suggestions are wrong." Casey's stance, hands on her waist, head tilted to one side, told of her exasperation.

Hunter grinned at her in a way that was becoming familiar but was no less appealing. He'd been like a different person since they'd talked, touching her from time to time and making no effort, if ever he had, to keep his eyes from her face. The smiles he gave her were very warm, and twice he'd asked her questions about how she'd coped with certain aspects of Nathan's death.

"Come on." He suddenly took her hand and began to run. "I know just the place."

Two minutes later Hunter was leading them inside the tool shed, more of a lean-to actually.

"Isn't this off limits?"

"Nope. It would be if it had a door. I was only hoping that Morgan hadn't beaten us to it."

Casey fell quiet. It was somewhat shadowy in this small building that smelled of oily rags and grass, and suddenly the atmosphere was rather close. Hunter must have felt it as well, because Casey looked up to find his eyes on her.

"I want to kiss you," he said in little more than a whisper.

Casey swallowed hard. "I think you're suddenly feeling things you haven't felt in a long time, Hunter, and I must admit to you that I've enjoyed our getting to know each other. But please," Casey's voice was tender, "be a little careful with my heart."

"Oh, Casey," Hunter's voice dropped unbelievably low. "I'm sorry if I've been totally insensitive to your feelings."

"You haven't," she said and then added very candidly, "but I've been alone for a long time, and I just wanted you to know that I'm not totally immune to you."

Hunter smiled, and Casey had the impression that her words pleased him no end. Their eyes held until the shouts of children in the distance broke the mood. Casey turned from Hunter and took a seat on an upturned, five-gallon paint bucket. They didn't talk anymore, but each one was very aware of the other's presence.

ɞ ɞ ɞ

"Thank you, Morgan," Casey said with a smile as Morgan hefted her basket of laundry from the car they'd borrowed to go into town. It was the weekend between the junior high and high school camps, and Casey and Morgan had just gone to wash clothes.

He'd driven the car as close as possible to the cabin, so it was an easy walk. When they arrived, Casey held the door to her cabin open so Morgan could take the basket inside. With that, Casey commented, "If you didn't have a girl waiting at home for you, Morgan, I'd marry you myself."

Morgan grinned like a boy. "You could always marry my brother."

Casey looked shocked. "What would Chris say?"

"You know very well that I'm not talking about Brad."

Casey only smiled and shook her head in feigned despair. "You've got to stop pushing Hunter and me together."

"But you would make him a wonderful wife," he told her seriously.

"Listen to yourself, Morgan. Your brother is a big boy, and I'm no kid myself. We can handle this on our own."

"I know he cares for you," Morgan went on as if he hadn't heard her. "I'm just afraid he's going to move too slowly and let you get away."

Casey didn't respond. She was afraid also but for an entirely different reason. Last weekend, when the fifth- and sixth-grade campers had gone home, she and Hunter had gone for a long walk in the woods. It had been a beautiful day, and they had even packed a lunch and taken a blanket so they could picnic under the trees. The day had seemed perfect: The food, their conversation, and the general spirit of their time together proved wonderful. It seemed even more perfect when Hunter had taken her into his arms and kissed her.

In the days that followed he'd been extremely attentive whenever they were alone and it was appropriate to be so. He'd even asked Casey out on a date for the next Saturday night, the Saturday that was today, but Casey's fears were not that he was moving too fast. They came from the fact that she could almost feel Gail between them. If Hunter showed up tonight still wearing his wedding band, Casey wasn't sure what she would do.

He'd held her hand numerous times, put his arm around her, and kissed her in the woods. It was becoming obvious that he no longer felt married, but if this was the case, why was he still wearing his wedding ring? Only Hunter knew.

"I think I've lost you," Morgan commented.

Casey smiled. "I have a date with Hunter tonight, Morgan, and I'm looking forward to going, but I mean it when I tell you that you've got to let us handle this on our own."

Morgan sighed. "All right, but if he lets you get away—"

"Even if he does," Casey cut him off, "it's still Hunter's business."

Morgan stared at her, clearly dissatisfied with the way his hands were tied, but Casey's serious expression told him he had better let the matter drop.

❧ ❧ ❧

Hours later, Casey, dressed in the nicest outfit she'd brought on tour, sat across the table from Hunter. They were in Santa Barbara's finest restaurant, and Hunter was making her feel like she was the most wonderful woman he'd ever met. If this was his attitude, the feelings were more than mutual for Casey. Even the sight of the ring on his hand couldn't completely dampen the pleasure she felt at being with Hunter Riley.

"How is your entree?" Hunter asked solicitously.

"Wonderful. How about yours?"

"Excellent."

They ate for a moment in silence, and then Hunter broached a question he hadn't been able to get off his mind.

"I want to ask you a question, Casey, but I'm afraid the subject might be upsetting to you."

"I'll be honest," she told him.

"It's about your daughter, Alison."

Casey smiled. "I appreciate your sensitivity, Hunter, but I never mind talking about her."

"How old would she be now?"

"About Linda's age, but in my mind she'll always be a baby." Casey smiled with remembrance. "She was such a happy child, so full of life. She was very active. Some days I fell into bed exhausted, but we didn't clash wills very often. She was very obedient most of the time. I think Alison would have been a people-pleaser.

"After the fire I thought I might be expecting again. I really struggled with God's will when I wasn't. I felt it would have been so right to have Nathan's child and Alison's little brother or sister, but I no longer feel that way. God's perfect plan is to have two parents. I know that many men and women do it on their own, but I'm thankful now that I'm not trying to raise a child by myself."

"I know it's a lot of work," Hunter told her. "My mother raised the four of us by herself."

Casey nodded. Janelle had told her, but she remained quiet.

"My father died when Morgan was four. My mother didn't remarry until just a few years ago, and of course by then we were all grown and out of the house."

"She must be a wonderful woman."

"I think so," Hunter told her honestly. "I'd like you to meet her sometime."

Casey had taken a bite of food and did not reply. She really didn't enjoy the mystery of a situation like this. She found herself fighting the impulse to read things into Hunter's comments, such as the one about meeting his mother. A double meaning had definitely come to mind. Had he meant more than just a casual statement? Once again, only Hunter knew.

"Hunter?" Casey called his name and waited until he looked at her. "How did your wife die?"

"Cancer. If I had known then what I know now, she would probably still be alive, but we took the doctor's word about waiting, and by the time the signs were really evident, it was all through her."

"You sound as though you have regrets."

"Not exactly. I know God's will is perfect, and we did our best, but sometimes it's hard to handle 'human error.' Do you know what I mean?"

"I think I do."

The meal ended in a companionable way, but as they drove back to camp, Casey felt a mix of emotions. It seemed they had so little time to get to know each other, and Casey honestly wanted to know this man. Some of her emotions must have shown on her face because Hunter said goodnight in a very quiet way and did not walk her all the way to her cabin. Casey had the impression that he wanted to but was thankful he held off.

She went to bed that night hoping that at the end of high school camp, when the family took a well-earned week of vacation, she and Hunter would finally have some quality time. However, this was not to be. Halfway through the week, Brad announced that the family had taken a vote. They were all so tired of being on the road that, to a person, they had elected to head straight home.

❧ ❧ ❧

As much as Casey dreaded leaving this family, she smiled at the sight of her car. There had been communication with the family at home, and Dan Green had seen to it that Casey's car was waiting for her in the designated spot.

Every one of the Rileys, save for Janelle and Dan, lived in Stockton. Dan, along with a friend, had left Casey's car in the church parking lot in Stockton so that Casey could drive home to Sacramento whenever the tour bus arrived. Her gear was unloaded rather solemnly, but when she and Chris finally stood together, they both grinned like children.

"It's been fun," Casey said.

"It has indeed," Chris agreed.

They hugged, and everyone gathered then to say goodbye and thank her for everything. Casey was equally grateful to them for the wonderful weeks they'd shared with her.

They didn't, however, linger overly long. They were all within minutes of home, but Casey had some miles to go. They let her go after just a few moments, with a promise from Morgan that she would get an invitation to the wedding and more promises from the others to visit when they came to see Dan and Janelle.

Casey picked up her small case, and no one moved to help or follow when Hunter threw Casey's bag over his shoulder and walked her to her car. Casey didn't look at Hunter as she opened the trunk to stow her gear or when she opened the driver's door, started the car without getting in, and put the air conditioning on full blast.

She let the door close softly and stepped slightly away from the hot metal of the door. The move put her almost directly in front of Hunter. He was literally on the verge of opening his mouth to tell her he would call, but Casey suddenly reached for his left hand.

Hunter stared downward, first at Casey's blonde, shiny head, and then as she fingered his ring. She didn't look at him or speak but turned the ring gently around his finger, her eyes on the movement. After a minute she looked up and said, "I hope you take care of yourself,

Hunter, and if you ever decide to take this ring off, give me a call."

Hunter was utterly speechless when she dropped his hand.

"Goodbye, Hunter."

All words deserted him as he watched Casey climb into her car and drive away with a small wave of her hand. He stood still for long minutes and finally lifted his left hand and stared at it as though it belonged to someone else. He thought then as he had many times, he'd never before met a woman like Casey Sheridan.

* * *

"How are you feeling?" Casey whispered to Janelle.

"Great."

"Oh, that's super." Casey's eyes shone. "I have to play for Loni, so I'm going to move down front, but I'll come over tonight and see you after church. Tell Dan to have popcorn ready."

"I'll do it. Are you going to the Hendersons' for lunch?"

Casey had time only to nod before she needed to move to her seat. She was settled before the announcements were made, and she never missed a beat when it was time to play, but her mind was elsewhere.

It had been six weeks since she'd seen Hunter, and he hadn't been in contact in any way. Not even when he'd spoken with Janelle did he pass on a word of greeting. Casey was not sorry for what she had said to him, but it was becoming painfully evident that he was not ready to remove that ring.

It was with great effort that Casey managed to pull her mind from Hunter and heed the sermon, but she was very glad that she did, since the pastor spoke on obedience to Christ, no matter what. Casey needed to hear those words right then. She was losing her joy over the whole ordeal with Hunter.

Pastor Meyer reminded them, "All of life's circumstances must be viewed through Christ, or we are going to spend our lives on an emotional roller coaster. Believing that God cares for us *only* when all is comfortable in our world makes for a shaky foundation, my friend. God's Word has to be our base. When it is, nothing, and I mean positively nothing, can cause the ground beneath us to shift."

It was just what Casey needed to hear. The summer had ended on a low note, and even going back to work had not been as joyful as it had other years. She now saw so plainly that her actions were telling God that He had let her down. Casey prayed right then with her new knowledge. She confessed her absorption with herself and surrendered her life and future to God.

Peace surrounded her for the first time in far too long. She was feeling nearly jubilant when church ended and Corrie Henderson approached her about lunch. Casey taught with Corrie's mom, Betty, and ate Sunday dinner with them most weeks, but since Corrie was a worrywart, she always checked with Casey.

"Are you coming over, Casey?"

Casey smiled at her and started to answer when she looked over the eight-year-old's head and spotted Hunter. He was across the near-empty foyer, and Casey couldn't think or move. She stared at him in something akin to confusion until he very deliberately reached up and scratched his chin with his *bare* left hand.

"Casey?"

"Oh! Corrie," she stumbled and thought fast. "You know, something has come up, and I won't be able to come today. Can you tell your mom?"

"Are you all right?" the little girl wanted to know.

"Yes," Casey answered with a beaming smile. "I'm just fine. Tell your mom I'll call her later."

Corrie was relieved when she saw that smile, and not having noticed Hunter, went off without a care. Casey then approached Hunter quite slowly and stopped.

"Hello." Hunter's voice was just as she remembered, deep and soft, and his eyes were just as warm.

"Hello, Hunter."

An awkward moment passed.

"Is there someplace we can talk?"

"We could go back to my apartment," Casey suggested.

Hunter nodded, and they moved to the door. Casey knew that the few remaining people watched her exit, but she didn't meet anyone's eyes. Once in the parking lot, Hunter followed her to her little yellow car.

"Did you drive?"

"Not to church."

"Oh, well." Again she felt at a loss. "Hop in."

Suddenly Casey couldn't remember how to drive. She fumbled with the clutch and nearly stalled the car twice before gaining the street. The ride to her apartment was a blur, and as soon as she let herself in the door, she crossed the room from Hunter and stood like a scared rabbit.

"Sit down," she offered, her voice breathless as she tried to control the pounding of her heart. However, Hunter remained standing. After a moment he said, "Casey, would you rather I hadn't come?"

"No, Hunter, no! I'm glad you're here."

"Then why are you so far away?" His gentle voice was nearly Casey's undoing, but she spoke with feigned calm.

"Because I think we need to talk before we touch." Where this had come from Casey couldn't have said. In reality she wanted to throw her arms around him, but in her heart she knew this was best.

Hunter nodded, thinking that her level head was one of the things he loved about her. He'd have laughed if he could have heard her thoughts.

When Hunter sat, Casey did also. Another small silence passed, but this one wasn't awkward. Hunter glanced around her apartment and commented on the lovely decor.

"I like it," Casey admitted. "It's not very big, but it's home."

"I've missed you, Casey," Hunter suddenly interjected.

Casey smiled, feeling more at ease by the moment. "I've missed you too. You took rather a long time to contact me."

Now Hunter smiled. "I'm sorry about that. Almost as soon as I got home I removed the ring, but I'd promised myself that our next meeting would be in person, not by phone or letter. Then life went nuts with tour wrap-up. I couldn't get away to come to you."

"But you're here now."

"Yes." Hunter smiled again. "I want to tell you that I'm here so we can get to know each other, and that would be true, but I've got to tell you right up front: My feelings for you are serious."

Casey stared at him for a moment and then looked away. She was silent for so long that Hunter shifted to see her face better and spoke again.

"What are you thinking, Casey?"

She took a big breath and admitted, "I've never felt for a man as I feel for you, Hunter, and it scares me." She turned her head to see him now. "I loved Nathan, but I was so young, and I see now what a selfish type of love it was. Now I'm feeling things I never thought I'd feel. No, that isn't true," Casey corrected herself. "I'm feeling things I didn't even know existed, and it's all a bit overwhelming."

Hunter lovingly held her gaze. "Since we're being totally up-front, I'll tell you that I'm head-over-heels where you are concerned."

Casey bit her lip.

"I'm not here to ask for your hand," he went on, "because you're not ready for that. But as I said before, my feelings are serious. Since your feelings are rather frightening to you, would you rather I stay, or would it be better if I left now?"

Casey's heart slowed to normal at that point, and things became very clear.

"I would like you to stay, but I will ask you the same thing I did before: Please be careful with my heart."

"That I can gladly do."

He spoke tenderly before he moved to the other end of the sofa, the one near her chair, and reached for her hand. Casey gave it gladly.

They talked for the next three hours until Hunter calmly announced to Casey that he was starving. With much laughter they raided Casey's refrigerator. Twenty minutes had passed when Hunter used a napkin to wipe whipped cream from the corner of her mouth. Casey knew in an instant that Hunter had refrained from kissing it off, and this restraint, more than anything he had said or done, told her that something wonderful was happening between them.

🌹 🌹 🌹

"It's not every brother who would come home early from his honeymoon for his sister," Hunter teased Janelle as she lay in the hospital bed.

Janelle smiled at him but didn't apologize. "Did you see her?"

"Yes," Casey told her. "And she's beautiful."

"She's awfully small, but the doctor says she's going to be all right."

"It's really your fault, Casey," Dan interjected.

"My fault?" She said with a laugh.

"That's right. If you had married Hunter on the first weekend he came into town, as I'm sure he wanted," Dan stressed, "early as she was, you'd have been back long before Deana was born."

"Can you believe that logic?" Casey asked her husband of eight days.

"Well, now," Hunter had caught Dan's teasing eye as he slipped an arm around Casey, "I think he might be right."

"Hopeless," Casey commented to Janelle and earned a wonderful smile, but she was teasing as well.

Dan leaned close to his wife just then, and Hunter took advantage of the time to kiss Casey. Casey melted in his arms and for the hundredth time thought about how she'd asked him to care for her heart, and how he'd done just that.

A Note from Lori: *When I was a teen, I had the opportunity to attend summer camp in northern California. On two different occasions I met singing groups from a Bible school in Michigan. I remembered the wonder I felt over the way the group sang and the fun they had together. Although "Be Careful With My Heart" does not strictly focus on the camp and singing groups, it was with those fond memories in mind that I wrote this story. By the way, I eventually attended the Bible school in Michigan, and that is where I met, fell in love, and became engaged to my husband, Bob Wick.*

Christmas for Two

Let your fountain be blessed,
and rejoice in the wife of your youth.
Proverbs 5:18

*E*llen Farling walked to the edge of the family room and stood very still. She could just see her husband's gray hair above the paper he held in front of his face. The evening had gone much as it always did. Dinner was over, the dishes were done, and they had taken an hour-long walk. Now they would settle in their comfortable chairs and read until the late news came on.

Ellen moved to her chair and picked up the book she was reading. The book remained unopened. Her eyes stared unseeingly at the back of Stan's newspaper, but he didn't notice. Feeling like a coward, Ellen sighed very gently and finally raised the book to her face.

"That was quite a sigh," Stan said softly, and Ellen shifted the book to see him peeking out at her. She'd have laid money on the fact that he hadn't even noticed her coming into the room; newspapers did that to him.

"I'm a coward," she admitted.

"About what?"

"About not talking to you."

Stan's brows rose. Their relationship was very open, and he didn't think Ellen had ever been afraid to come to him.

"Have I done something?"

"No, it's nothing like that."

Stan waited, but Ellen didn't continue. Stan folded the paper and set it aside. Ellen wasn't certain that she wanted to have the discussion right now, but it was too late; he was looking at her expectantly, his face kind and open.

Ellen felt terrible for making it sound as though it was his fault that she couldn't talk to him. He didn't even know what she was referring to. She took a breath and plunged in.

"It's about Christmas."

Stan nodded with instant understanding.

"I knew it would come to this, Stan, and I'm fine with it. I mean, all children grow up and establish their own lives, but our being here alone is hard for me. I've even considered the different people we could invite from the church, but with all three kids gone, I thought this might be the year we could do something special, just you and me."

Stan remained silent, but he knew where she was headed; he knew exactly what she wanted to do.

"Why would you be afraid to ask me?"

"Because you're such a traditionalist," she said, not unkindly.

"That's true," he admitted, knowing how correct she was.

For years Ellen had been asking if they could go to Disneyland for Christmas—not just on the kids' break from school—but on Christmas Day. Stan and the kids had never agreed. Christmas in the Rocky Mountains, with the towering snowcapped mountains that surrounded their home in Colorado Springs, was like something out of a storybook. Stan and the three kids had never been willing to part with the snow and the Christmas morning traditions around the tree. Ellen had never put up a fuss, and she didn't ask every year, but Stan knew better than anyone how badly she wanted to go.

"You hate the idea as much as you always have—I can see it in your face."

"No, I don't, Ellen, but Bunny," he said, referring to their daughter who was still in college, "wasn't certain whether she could be here or not, remember? I think we'd feel terrible if she decided to come home and we had made plans to be away."

"You're right," Ellen agreed graciously, but Stan was swamped with guilt. All these years and she never complained. She would ask, maybe in October or at Thanksgiving, if they could consider it, but she never once argued or pushed the point.

"Now that I think about it," Ellen added, "I haven't even looked at the money side of it. I'm not sure we could swing it this year." Her voice told of her acceptance. There was not even a hint of resignation, and again guilt flooded Stan. He had received a healthy bonus on his last paycheck, and he'd completely forgotten to tell her. However, the guilt was easily put aside when he thought of Bunny wanting to come and their not being there. If he knew for certain that they would be alone, he would look into it, but as it was, he felt he had no choice.

"Are you terribly disappointed?" he asked.

"No," she told him honestly, but she realized right after she said it that she was disappointed and very tired. She knew that this would be the last time. They'd been married for 27 years. The first time she had asked was before their third Christmas together, when the twins had been only a year old. It was time to let the dream go. It wasn't as if they had never gone to Disneyland, but it was Ellen's favorite place, and Christmas was her favorite holiday.

Lost in thought, she eventually picked up her book and began to read. Stan picked up his paper as well, but Ellen wasn't aware of the way his eyes lingered on her for quite some time.

🌷 🌷 🌷

"You look thoughtful," Stan's coworker commented to him a few days later, and Stan looked at her as she stood in the doorway of his office. Bethany had not been with the firm very long, but she was a valuable asset.

"I was thinking about Christmas."

"Ah," she said knowingly. "Bud and I just had that out last night."

"You make it sound like a fight."

"These days, it is. It's funny—isn't the mother supposed to be the one who longs to be with her children?"

"But you don't?"

"It's not that I don't want to see them, Stan, but I don't have to see them to have a good Christmas. Bud does. I figure it has to do with the way Bud traveled when the children were growing up while I stayed home. I didn't go back to school until they were all out of the house, so I don't look back with any regrets. I think Bud feels he missed something and is trying to make up for it now."

"What would you want to do?"

"Just stay home and not drive to the kids'. Bud's mother always joins us, and I think the three of us would have a great time."

"So the kids don't come home to you?"

She shook her head. "Not since we moved into the condo; there's not enough room. We usually gather at Katie's in Denver. She'd have a fit if we didn't come, but it would be worth it to me. We'll all be going there for Thanksgiving, but I'm definitely ready to stay home for Christmas this year."

Stan could hardly believe what he was hearing. Why did he think that his wife was the only one who wanted to break tradition? Bethany ached to be at home, even if it meant not being with her children. He knew she had grandchildren, but evidently she could even take a break from them this year.

"So what was the decision?" Stan asked from his desk, knowing it was time to get back to work.

"We're going," she said simply as she moved away from the door, but Stan noticed that there was nothing in her voice—no anger and no joy. Ellen had not sounded resigned, but her face had looked so weary.

What about the kids? Stan's mind argued. *Bunny might be coming.* But the fight fell flat in his thinking before it could even get started. Yes, he loved Bunny, his twin daughters, Jen and Rene, their husbands, and even his

little grandson, Ethan, and he praised God for them,
but hadn't Ellen been there first? It was a question Stan
wrestled with for several days. Ellen was as normal as
could be, but Stan was in a quandary.

❧ ❧ ❧

The sun was shining through the window, and even
though Ellen knew the laundry and grocery shopping
awaited her, she sat with another cup of coffee. Her
Bible was open in front of her, but her eyes were on the
snow and the way it sparkled in the early sunlight.
After a moment she prayed softly.

"I've been selfish, Lord, just thinking of what I
want. I shouldn't have said anything to Stan about
Disneyland. He was so quiet last night, and he's been
preoccupied for a few days. I think I made him feel terrible by bringing it up. Lay the people on my heart,
Lord, the families You would have us reach out to.
Maybe the Bickleys or the Johns. I know Stan would
have a good time with them too. You planned all this,
Lord. You knew that this would be our first Christmas
alone, and You also know just how You want us to
spend it. It's going to be wonderful, Lord. We won't see
Ethan this year, but we can invite a couple with little
ones and delight in them."

Her heart at great peace knowing God was going to
give them a blessed time, Ellen reached for a piece of
paper. She would jot down the names of a few families
and run them past Stan when he got home tonight.
They would invite whomever he wanted. It didn't
matter because Ellen knew that it would be planned by
the Lord.

❧ ❧ ❧

"Hi, Dad." Bunny's voice sounded cheerful on the other end of the line, the connection good for long distance.

"Hi, honey." Stan answered, pleasantly surprised. "What's up?"

She rarely called the office, which only added to the delight of hearing from her.

"My plans for London fell through. I tried to call Mom, but there was no answer. I'm just calling to let you know that I'll be home after all and probably bringing one of my roomies with me."

"Oh." Stan's lack of enthusiasm immediately caught his daughter's attention. If she could have seen him, she would have also noticed the way his hand sought a business-size envelope on his desk.

"Is something wrong, Dad?"

"No," he said quietly—and knew in an instant that it wasn't. "It's just that your mother and I won't be home for Christmas."

Stan was met with silence. Dead silence.

"What did you say?" Bunny finally asked in a voice so unbelieving that Stan was shamed.

"I said we won't be home," his voice carrying more conviction with every word. "As much as we'd like to see you, do you suppose you could ask Rene or Jenny if you could hunker in with them for that day and the few days around Christmas?"

"Dad," Bunny's voice took on a teasing quality, "are you running a fever? You should probably be lying down."

Stan laughed.

"Where will you be?" Bunny asked when he quieted.

"Disneyland."

"Oh, Dad. I can't believe it. Are you serious?"

"Very serious."

"Oh, Dad," she said again.

"Bunny, are you crying?"

"Yes, I'm crying! Mom's wanted to go for so long, and we never did." She sniffed loudly. "I just think it's so neat."

Stan found himself well-pleased with his decision.

"When are you going?"

"We fly out on the twenty-third and come back the twenty-seventh. You can still come home, you know," he added. "We just won't be there."

"I'll come. Right after you get back, I'll come. Oh, Dad..." She was crying again, and Stan knew he would have to get off or he'd be bawling too.

"What did she say when you told her?"

"I haven't."

"When are you going to?"

"Tonight."

"All right. I'll let Jen know, and she can call Rene, but we'll all stay quiet until we hear from you."

They rang off just a few minutes later, but Bunny's comments were so heavy on his mind that Stan couldn't concentrate. He did his best to finish up what he was working on and went home for the day.

❧ ❧ ❧

"Well!" Ellen smiled with pleasure and went to kiss Stan as he came through the kitchen door. "Home early. This is a nice surprise."

He smiled, slipped his arms around her, and returned her kiss. "I thought we might go to dinner, and I wanted to catch you before you started something." *I also had to see your face and hold you because I love you so much,* he thought, but these were words he couldn't say out loud.

"Out to dinner! How fun. My hair was strange today. Will I look all right?"

"You'll be beautiful."

His tone was so serious that Ellen stopped touching her hair and looked at him. He smiled hugely at her, and they kissed again. He then sent her off with a swat to her blue-jeaned backside.

"Go now. We'll leave when you're ready."

Ellen didn't have to be asked twice. She obediently headed to their bedroom, slipped into one of her good Sunday dresses, and joined her husband just as fast as she could.

🌱 🌱 🌱

The meal was lovely, simple and delicious, and they talked of everything but Christmas. They had gone out early, so the evening was young when they headed to the car.

"Are you up to a little shopping?"

"Shopping? Stan, are you feeling well?"

He laughed but didn't answer, and Ellen was in the car before she took him seriously. He headed straight for the mall. Though not yet Thanksgiving, the mall was already filled with Christmas decorations. Even the air seemed festive with the season. They walked for a time, holding hands and not sharing too much until Stan headed them toward a bench. They sat, Stan's arm along the back of the bench behind Ellen's shoulders. They were content to sit with their own thoughts and watch people pass.

Finally Stan commented, "Bunny called me at the office today."

"At the office? Is she all right?"

"She's fine. She'd tried you at home and couldn't reach you."

"It must have been when I was at the market. What did she need?"

"Her plans for London have fallen through. She wants to come home for Christmas and bring a friend."

"Is she terribly disappointed?"

"I don't think so."

"Well, it will be wonderful to have her. Who's she bringing?"

"She didn't have a chance to tell me because I told her we wouldn't be here."

Ellen stared at him and watched as he took an envelope from his pocket. He placed it in her lap. Ellen's hand went to her mouth when she saw the travel agent's name in the corner.

"Oh, Stanley," she breathed. "What have you done?"

"Have you changed your mind?"

"No, but I had completely shifted gears. I even have a list of names at home—people we could ask to join us for Christmas."

"Have you already asked them?"

She shook her head. "I wanted to check with you first."

"Then there's really no harm done."

"But Bunny, what did she say?"

"She cried."

"Oh, Stan, no."

"She did. She thought it was the neatest thing. Said you'd been asking for years and how proud she was of me that I would break tradition."

Stan's arm brought her close now, and Ellen buried her face in his neck. Stan didn't know what to say. His heart was so full. He wanted to tell Ellen how much she meant to him, how sorry he was that he'd never taken her before, and that this act was so small compared to all he felt inside. But the words would not come.

Holding her near, however, the smell and feel of her hair so close to his face, he glanced down to the envelope still in her lap. He couldn't say the words right now, but maybe he didn't have to.

❧ ❧ ❧

The waitress put the plates in front of them, and both Ellen and Stan bowed their heads so Stan could pray. Stan had just put his napkin in his lap when Ellen leaned close.

"We did it. We're in Disneyland on Christmas Day."

Stan chuckled. "That we did. What do you want to ride first?"

"Thunder Mountain Railroad," she said without hesitation.

"And second?"

Ellen didn't know. She was too excited to think beyond that. Every time they visited the Magic Kingdom, they ate breakfast in a restaurant that served early birds before the main street opened. That's where they were now: eating alone in Disneyland, no children for the first time, and on Christmas Day.

"We'll have to bring Ethan with us sometime, but I'm so glad we're here alone," Ellen confided.

"Me too," Stan agreed before leaning toward her to share a pancake-syrup kiss.

Watching them from two tables away, a very young couple looked at each other and smiled.

"Do you think they're honeymooners like we are?" the young woman asked.

"Too old," the young man proclaimed.

"I don't know." She was clearly skeptical as she watched Ellen's adoring eyes on Stan. "They act like honeymooners." She turned back to her new husband. "Are you still going to kiss me when we're that old?"

The man's eyes twinkled. "What do you think?"

The two shared another smile, and both glanced back at the other table. The main street to Disneyland had been open for about ten minutes, but the man and woman with the graying hair were still sitting very close, noses nearly touching, and talking as though they had all the time in the world.

A Note from Lori: *I wrote this story not long after I lost my father and wept buckets in the process, but it's really not about my parents. Much as I love the holidays in snowy Wisconsin, someday I would love for Bob and me to flaunt convention and run away to Disneyland on Christmas Day. And who knows? Maybe someday we'll do just that.*

The Haircut

The last day of school, usually so exciting for Bobby, was tempered a bit by a trip to the barber. The weeks between Easter vacation and the end of school had stretched on endlessly for Bobby as his older siblings went off to school each day, but now his brothers and sisters would be home for the rest of the summer, and he would have full-time playmates. If only his mother hadn't spoiled the excitement just after breakfast.

"The kids will be home at half past eleven," she had said, "so we'd better get downtown. I need to pick up the mail, get milk and bread, and stop at the hardware store. Although," she paused a moment, "you need to get to the barber, so we'll do that first."

"The barber?" he'd asked in dismay, but his mother was poring over her list and didn't reply.

Less than an hour later, Bobby's mother's words came to fruition, and he found himself in the barber's chair, cranked high into the air, the sound of the clippers assailing his small ears.

It's best for everyone reading Bobby's story to understand something about Wisconsin in the early 1960's—little boys had butch haircuts. A butch was short and fuzzy. There was nothing left to brush or style, since all the hairs of the head were the same short length.

Bobby didn't care for this style, but as a five-year-old, his opinion on the matter counted for little. His brother Johnny was three years older, but he could not sway his mother's beliefs either. If Bobby's guess was right, Johnny would be downtown the next morning for his own shearing.

At the moment, however, Bobby sat pragmatically before the huge mirror as Les and his electric clippers did their job. The result was much the same as all the haircuts before, and no one noticed the small sigh that lifted the red-striped cover swathing Bobby's small form.

❧ ❧ ❧

Weeks later the family left the state for their traditional summer vacation. Bobby smiled secretly to himself as his hand reached surreptitiously for the hair at the back of his head. In all the bustle and rush of vacation plans and packing, no one had taken time to get the younger boys to the barber for a late summer haircut. Bobby knew very well that the barber shop would be their first stop when they arrived back home, but in the meantime, he had more hair on his head than he'd had in a long time.

Bobby's joy, however, was short-lived. After they'd settled their travel trailer into a campground in Georgia, Mother told Bobby's older sister Jane to walk the boys into town for haircuts. Bobby was quiet as they ambled along, hoping in his heart that the town wouldn't have a barber.

Once on the short city streets, some of Bobby's chagrin deserted him. Fascinated, he took in the clapboard storefronts of an unfamiliar town. He saw a five-and-ten-cent store, a bank, two small grocery stores, a small hardware store, a clothing emporium, a real estate office—and a barber shop.

Bobby spotted this last establishment without much enthusiasm, but he marched obediently across the threshold when Jane held the door. The barber was friendly enough, and the change in shops was interesting, but Bobby still felt a bit cheated.

"Well, now," the barber offered as he put down the weekly paper and stood. "What can I do for you today?"

"My brothers need haircuts," Jane told him with calm efficiency.

"Well, who'll be first?"

With that question, Bobby climbed into the chair and lifted his chin for the drape. He stared at himself in the mirror and just barely heard the conversation between the barber and his sister.

"Just a trim today?"

"The barber at home always gives them a butch."

"A butch?" the barber asked with some confusion.

Jane's hands gestured around her own head. "It's just cut short all over."

"With the clippers?"

"Yes, that's right."

The barber nodded and switched the clippers on. His first sweep, straight back from the front of Bobby's head, made Bobby's little heart sink with dread. In the seconds that followed, a boy appeared in the mirror that Bobby had never seen before: He was nearly bald.

The contrast between his tan face and white scalp was startling. Bobby's mind went back to a picture he'd seen once in *National Geographic*. The photo had accompanied a story covering the last world war and depicted a group of pathetic-looking refugees, their hair as short as his own.

It was a somber five-year-old who climbed down from the barber's chair. Bobby knew he should thank the barber, but the words would not come. It didn't help to look over at Jane and see her eyes wide with shock.

Within minutes Johnny looked as much like a war victim as Bobby, and after Jane paid the man, they went on their way. Bobby never would have believed that one-quarter of an inch could make such a difference, but he felt so bare that he was tempted to run all the way back to camp.

❧ ❧ ❧

Bobby's mother had little to say when they came back but hugged each boy, thanked Jane, and gave all five of her children some lunch. Bobby stuck his tongue out at his other sister, Margaret, when he caught her staring at him. He simply ignored his oldest brother, Jeff. However, the afternoon passed in good fun. They swam and played, and for a time Bobby forgot about his bald head.

That evening over supper at the big picnic table outside their trailer, Bobby's dad was quieter than usual. Bobby caught him watching him from time to time, and he frantically searched his mind to see if he might be in trouble over something.

The meal ended, and while his mother was doing the dishes inside, his father entered the trailer. Bobby sat on the rear bed coloring in a book.

"Helen, it's about time those boys had some hair on their heads," he said without preamble.

"It is awfully short, John," she agreed. "But you know Les never cuts it that close." Mother's hands dripped with soapy water as she shifted to face him.

"No matter," he spoke decisively. "No more butches."

Mother agreed without an argument, and after a moment, without looking in the direction of the little boy at the rear of the trailer, they both laughed softly. Father then made his way back outside.

Bobby watched him go from his place back on the bed. He moved to the edge of the double mattress and leaned out precariously into what would have been considered the hallway to the rear of the trailer. On the back of the bathroom door was a mirror, one that would have been over his head if his feet had been on the floor. By stretching just so, he was able to see himself in that mirror.

Staring back at him was the same bald-headed little boy he'd seen in the barber shop. This time, however, there was something different: This time was to be the last.

Bobby grinned at himself in the glass before going back to his coloring book, thinking as he did, *I should have thanked the barber after all.*

A Note from Lori: *I married the little boy in this story, and even though "Bobby" still goes for haircuts, there is now far less to cut. It was a fun story to hear, and also fun to write about my husband's immediate family. I will admit that I took some literary license. I did not, however, change names to protect the innocent.*

Beyond the Picket Fence

An excellent wife, who can find?
For her worth is far above jewels.
Proverbs 31:10

❧❧❧

I can't think why you want to do this," her editor had said, but she wouldn't listen.

"I've never liked New York City," she had told him as she continued to pack. "And then the house I was raised in, the one in Pine Tree, Vermont, went on the market. I just bought it; we closed the deal this afternoon."

"But you don't even have family left there." The elegantly dressed editor had looked stunned.

"That doesn't matter. It's a great town with a super church. I've made up my mind, Monty," she said, facing him squarely. "I'm going to move home and write my books there."

That had been just two short months ago. Now, Dominique J. Brinks, "Nikki" to nearly everyone, stood looking at her spacious living room, boxes piled everywhere, and wondered at her own sanity. It had sounded so ideal, but the whole point had been to leave the mad rush of New York City behind and have time to write. She wondered if she could even find her computer in all of this. There was a box marked "computer," but she had found office supplies inside. In the midst of her tumultuous thoughts, the doorbell rang. Nikki waded her way to the door and found a man from the phone company on the step.

"Am I ever glad to see you," she told him as he came across the threshold.

"Most people feel that way," he said with a smile. "Where do you want me to begin?"

Nikki showed him the place in her bedroom upstairs, the area where she wanted a phone in the kitchen, and the spot in the spacious dining room off the kitchen. The house wasn't huge, but she knew she would spend the majority of her time in those three areas, and it was easier to install three phones than to wander around with a cordless and forget where she last left it.

Since the house had had phone lines before, the man didn't need much time, and Nikki was thrilled when he handed her the local phone book and her new number. He said he'd already called into the office and everything was working fine. In a burst of pleasure, her hands shaking a little with excitement, Nikki dialed the local library and listened to a recording about its hours. She then tried a few more numbers and went back to her unpacking.

As much as she wanted to get settled in the bedroom and kitchen so she felt really moved in, her feet drove her toward the dining room and her huge task there. She couldn't stand all the boxes stacked around, so she cleared the room until only the furniture was left.

At that point she began opening the needed boxes in the living room and carrying her things to the dining room. She hung pictures, positioned odds and ends, and each time stood back and smiled at her efforts. She was finally ready for the most important addition and was dragging it carefully from the living room when the front doorbell rang.

Sure that the telephone man had forgotten something, she swung the door wide before realizing who stood before her.

"Mother!" she cried with joy and threw her arms around an older version of herself. "I just tried to call you."

"Well, I'm not home," Virginia Warburton told her with a satisfied smile. "I'm headed to see my daughter in Vermont."

"Oh, Mom." Nikki could have cried but didn't. "Is Tim with you?"

"He's here in town but not with me right now. I think he wanted to give us a little time alone."

"I'm so glad you're here."

"Well," her mother's tone became firm. "I'm not here for fun. I'm here to help you move in."

"Are you really?"

"Of course. Nearly all your friends from here have moved away, and I knew you'd be on your own."

"I won't turn that offer down. Come and see what I've done."

Nikki led the way to the dining room and stood back.

"Oh, Nikki," her mother said softly. "This is wonderful. You told me you were going to set up your office in here, but I never imagined..."

"I just have to set up my computer, and I'm ready to go."

Virginia could only stare. Nikki's desk sat so that her back was to the main wall. To her left were windows and to her right was the door into the hall. The wall in front of her held the door back to the kitchen. Built-in shelves already sported books and writing awards. Nikki had had the covers of all her books framed. They now hung around the room, interspersed with cartoons and family photos. The effect was wonderful: a room not originally intended for anything but dining, but perfect nonetheless.

Virginia took a slow look around, the memories coming back. The nostalgia within these walls was very dear. The dining room had always been the family's favorite room. The huge bay windows that looked out over the acres of pines drew her close, and for a moment she stood quietly at the glass.

"Such memories, Nikki. It's no wonder you want to work right here."

"Remember the Christmas you broke your toe but still insisted on going with us to get the tree?"

Her mother chuckled. "Yes. I thought I'd die of cold before we found a tree we wanted."

"Dad was in a panic, sure that your exposed toe would be frostbitten, and we couldn't quit laughing."

"He wasn't too happy with us," Virginia agreed, but she couldn't stop the laugh that escaped her. Dominic Brinks had been dead for more than ten years, but the memory of that day was still strong in their minds.

"Well, now," Virginia piped as she turned from the window. "I think we'd better get to work. Where do you want to begin?"

"I think the upstairs. Are you and Tim going to stay here with me?"

"If you have a place for us to sleep."

"In that case, we'd better get started on the bedrooms."

With that, the women were off. The house had been left clean, but the movers had tracked in a certain amount of debris, so they dusted, vacuumed, moved furniture—usually several times—hung pictures, made beds, filled closets, and washed windows. They made themselves stay in a room until it was completely in order. Two of the three upstairs bedrooms were finished, as were both bathrooms, before they allowed themselves to move downstairs to the living room and kitchen.

Hours later, both thinking they could drop with exhaustion, they called it quits. They had no more collapsed on the sofa and love seat in the living room, when the front door opened.

"Hello," a cheerful male voice called, and Nikki summoned up just enough energy to meet her stepfather at the door.

"Hello, Tim," she said warmly as they hugged.

"How's my Nikki?" he asked, a tender light in his eyes. A widower with four children of his own, he still had room in his heart to adore his wife's only child.

"Tired and hungry, but so glad to be here."

Tim kissed her cheek a second time and reached for the bag he'd set down just inside the door.

"How does dinner sound?"

"Oh, Mom," Nikki called to her. "Tim brought fried chicken."

"You are an angel," Virginia declared as she came to join the fun. "We're so tired and hungry we thought we might just go to bed." She kissed his cheek and welcomed his hug.

"Help has arrived," he said kindly. "The kitchen or the dining room?"

"We'll let you decide," Virginia said calmly, looking forward to her husband's reaction. Tim's response was all they could hope for. He proclaimed with delight that his own office could never compare to Nikki's.

They ate with much thanks and fellowship, and as Virginia had predicted, they made an early night of it. They rose early, however, and worked steadily for the next two days.

Tim did handyman repairs, changing light bulbs and checking locks. He gave the furnace a good going-over and also did some work on the kitchen and bathroom sinks. After a huge list was compiled and purchased at the grocery store, the women continued with boxes of books, linens, and dozens of odds and ends.

Nikki spent some time with her computer and fax machine, and by the time the Warburtons took their leave, Nikki was well and truly settled. She said goodbye to them but without a hint of sadness. Their visit had been a complete surprise, and she had enjoyed every moment, but it was time to return to her writing.

❧ ❧ ❧

Two weeks later, Nikki sat back in her chair and rubbed her throbbing temples. She had been writing nonstop for days. It was time to take a break. Late summer in Vermont was very beautiful, but Nikki was missing it. She had a deadline to meet on this manuscript, but right now she had to have a rest. As it was a warm day, she was already dressed in shorts. She saved her current work on the computer, went for the walking shoes in her bedroom closet, and headed out the front door, the key in her pocket.

The house in which Nikki had grown up sat on a long stretch of road that sported only three homes. The road dead-ended into a beautiful meadow filled with maple trees and pines. That land belonged to the next house up the road. It was a huge white sprawling place with two stories and a large wraparound porch. The third house, another large structure, was out on the main street that led into town.

As a child she had played in the valley with the other children who lived on the street, but now she didn't know who owned the other homes. She began to walk toward the valley but wondered if someone might think her trespassing; one never knew these days. With that she started up the road, head bent against the wind, and forced her mind to empty itself of all but the Lord. She was thinking of His attributes, naming them one by one, when a small voice interrupted her reflection.

"Hello."

Nikki pulled up in surprise. She was on the far side of the large white house, nearly halfway down the road, when she turned to find a small girl.

"Hello," Nikki said right back, a friendly smile on her face.

"What's your name?" the little person standing off the road asked, cutting right to the chase.

"I'm Nikki. What's your name?"

"Petra. I'm not supposed to talk to strangers."

Nikki's smile widened, knowing it would do no good to remind the child that she had initiated the conversation. Instead she said, "I think you're very wise not to do that, but if your mom will let you, you can come and visit me. I live in the small house at the end of the road, beyond the picket fence."

Nikki watched her eyes shift down the road and back to her before saying goodbye. She could almost feel the child's eyes on her, but she didn't look back; neither did the child speak again. Nikki walked swiftly all the way up the road and back. It wasn't much of a workout, but it helped remove the webs from her mind and kinks from her neck. By the time she reached the big white house again, the child was gone, but Nikki thought about her as she went back to work, figuring she must have been about five or six, a little young for the books Nikki wrote, but still such a fun age.

Back at her desk, Nikki shifted her mind back onto the screen in front of her and read the last line of type.

With that she was immersed in the story again and didn't take a break until hours after dark.

❧ ❧ ❧

"Hello," the woman on the other end of the phone line offered tentatively, "I'm looking for Nikki Brinks."

"This is Nikki Brinks."

"Oh, Nikki, it's Shelly Marks. Do you remember me?"

"Of course I do, Mrs. Marks. How nice to hear from you." Shelly Marks was the mother of an old friend of Nikki's, one who had gone to high school with her.

"Well, dear, I hope you'll think so after I tell you why I called."

She sounded so worried that Nikki chuckled softly. "What can I do for you?"

"It's such late notice, Nikki, and I haven't seen you for years. I'm just so afraid you'll feel I'm taking advantage."

"That's nice of you, Mrs. Marks. I appreciate that, but if I can't help, I'll be the first to tell you."

"You'll be completely honest?"

"Yes, I will."

"Well, it's like this. You may remember that we have a small pet fair and contest every year, and, well, it's tied into the town's annual Maple Days celebration. Our vet, Dr. Borden, always does the judging, but the poor man has just been kicked by a cow and has broken his leg."

"How painful. Is he going to be all right?"

"Yes, but he'll be laid up for several days, and he's in a good deal of pain."

"I'm sorry to hear that. Is the fair soon?" Nikki had had her nose to the grindstone and had not been reading the local paper.

"This Saturday."

Today was Thursday, but Nikki didn't have to look at her calendar to know she had nothing scheduled.

"It's such late notice." Mrs. Marks was still apologizing.

"As a matter of fact," Nikki replied, "short notice is sometimes easier. What would you want me to do?"

"It's just for fun, Nikki," she began to explain. "The children bring their pets—we always see quite a variety—and you need to judge and award the first-, second-, and third-place ribbons."

Nikki saw more than Mrs. Marks was saying. She didn't have a pet when she was growing up, but there was a vague remembrance of this event. As arbiter, she would be expected to judge equally between dogs and goldfish, cats and pet turtles. It wasn't impossible, just challenging. She did, however, have one question.

"Why me, Mrs. Marks?"

"Because many of the children love to read your books." The older woman's voice grew warm. "A few of the teachers told me they were ecstatic when they heard you'd moved back into town."

There were times when Nikki was still surprised at how well-known her work was becoming, and this was one of them.

"Do you need to think about it, Nikki?" Mrs. Marks had misunderstood her silence. "I would understand."

"Not this time, I don't. I'd be glad to help out."

"Wonderful." The word was breathed with fervent relief. "The judging begins at one o'clock. Will that work for you?"

"Absolutely."

The remainder of the conversation covered where the competition would be held and who would be there to assist her. Nikki took some notes, thinking it sounded like fun. As soon as the ribbons were awarded, her duties would be over. Nikki hung up, still thinking it sounded like an adventure but also a little curious as to just what she'd gotten herself into.

❧ ❧ ❧

Pine Tree's community center was a beautiful structure. Just five years old, it was a far cry from the small gymnasium they had used when Nikki was a child. A spiral of excitement filling her, Nikki climbed from her car and started toward the door. She walked down the hallway that led to the auditorium, already able to hear the sound of many voices and the occasional bark of a dog.

She opened the front door, stepped inside, and was delighted to see she'd been wrong about the organization. Animals and children were everywhere, but with a few moments of observation, she could see that there *was* some order. It looked as if small pets—turtles, mice, rats, and such—were lined up along the left wall. In front of the stage were the cats, and to the right were the dogs. Nikki stood taking it all in until she saw Shelly Marks headed her way.

"Nikki," she called and then embraced her warmly. "Thank you for doing this."

"It's my pleasure. Where do I start?"

"Over here on the right with the dogs. You'll need to pick ribbons for each group."

"So in this first line I judge dogs only against dogs?"

"That's right. We changed the old rule a few years back. Against the stage are bunnies and cats, and then on the left it varies widely. I will tell you that we do have a few extra ribbons, so we can do a tie if you really can't decide. Anyone who doesn't place in the top three receives a purple ribbon for participation. Oh, there's my husband at the microphone now. He's ready to get things started." Nikki followed Mrs. Marks as she moved toward her spouse.

"Okay, folks, we're ready to get started now. If I could have a little quiet, I'll give you some instructions. Stay in line until our judge has seen all of the pets and dismisses your section with the raise of her hand." Nikki watched Mr. Marks smile and glance her way and tried not to blush when it became clear that he was going to introduce her.

"For those of you who haven't heard, I guess I should mention that Doc Borden is laid up with a broken leg, but Pine Tree's own published author, Nikki Brinks, has agreed to fill in for us." Mr. Marks paused. "We know Doc will be back with us next year, and we appreciate him, but it's no contest as to which judge is prettier."

As the room erupted with laughter and a few wolf whistles, Nikki felt herself go red from the neck up. She couldn't stop herself from wondering how in the world she could have been tempted to move back.

"Okay, now," barked Mr. Marks, restoring order. "After your section has been judged, you can move around some, but don't bother the other animals that are still waiting for Nikki. Let's all give Nikki a nice big welcome and get ready for a great time."

When they applauded, Nikki waved her hand briefly and started toward the first dog in the line. The next 20 minutes passed in what felt like seconds. She watched dog tricks, heard the dogs' names, and met all their owners. Nikki made notes on the pad Mrs. Marks had given her concerning every animal before moving on to the cats. Again she made notes as she met animals and owners alike. Doing her best not to look ahead, Nikki was surprised to come to the end of the second line and find her neighbor, a small rabbit in her arms.

"Well, Petra. I didn't know you had a pet."

The little girl nodded. "It's a rabbit."

"I see that. Does it have a name?"

"Fluffy," Petra told her, and Nikki wrote the name on her pad.

"And what is your last name, Petra?"

"Swann."

"Is the bunny a boy or a girl?" Nikki asked as she wrote.

"I think it's a girl."

Again, Nikki made note. "Do you take care of Fluffy yourself, Petra?"

She nodded and shifted the small scrap of gray fur a little closer to her chest. Nikki smiled at her, nothing unusual—she'd been smiling at children since she arrived—but this one was special.

Nikki asked a few more questions about Fluffy, thanked Petra, and then turned to go up the lefthand side of the room. The first pet was in a deep cardboard box on a small folding table. Nikki stepped up to the box, a smile on her face, but visibly started and gasped when she saw what was inside.

"A snake!" She tried to recover her smile, even as her skin crawled. "Your pet is a snake."

"Yes," the little boy standing behind the box spoke confidently. "His name is Brutus."

"Brutus," Nikki repeated, sounding winded even to her own ears. She took a moment to compose herself and forced her eyes into the box. A shiver ran over her, but she still asked the little boy's name.

"Theo Swann. Petra is my sister."

"Oh, how nice, Theo, uhm, tell me, what type of snake is Brutus?"

"He's a ribbon snake."

She wrote, but her hand shook noticeably. Again she made herself look into the box, and the snake chose that moment to slither his tongue out and move a little. Nikki felt transfixed with horror until she realized Theo was talking to her.

"He eats mice mostly, and I take care of him myself."

Nikki nodded and made herself write. *You've got to calm down, Dominique. Get a grip.*

"How long have you had him?"

"About six months."

Nikki glanced down to see the snake's tongue come out again but made herself stay calm.

"How often do snakes stick their tongues out, Theo?" This time she really wanted to know.

Theo told her what he'd studied on the subject and gave a very thorough accounting. Nikki thanked him sincerely, made herself look once more, and moved on.

Had she but bothered to look, she might have noticed the man who stood in the corner between the children. His eyes had barely left her since she'd started the judging, and after watching her with the snake, he wanted to howl with laughter. But Nikki never did glance his way. She was too busy with the last part of the small-animal lineup.

At last the judging was finished. She completed her list and handed it to Mr. Marks.

"I have our winners," he spoke into the mike. The crowd came forward in a bunch. "When your name is called, come up and Nikki will give you your ribbon. Everyone will receive a participation ribbon, but we'll hand out the first-, second-, and third-place ribbons first. You all did a great job, and I'm proud of you."

"Okay, for the dogs, third place goes to . . ."

The list was disposed of neatly. There was one tie among the dog ranks, and Nikki watched in pleasure as little faces lit up and families cheered. Telling herself it was just because they were her neighbors, she'd been watching Theo and Petra Swann. She felt her heart swell over Theo's excitement about a blue ribbon, but she had to turn away from Petra's tear-filled eyes when the little girl realized that Fluffy had not placed.

Mr. and Mrs. Marks rescued her by coming over to thank her for all her work. They pressed a schedule of events into her hands in case she hadn't seen the weekend's activities in The *Sap*, originally called the *Saturday Afternoon Paper*, and invited her to join them if she came to the barbecue that night. Nikki thanked them, not sure of her immediate plans.

She climbed back into her car, wondering when she'd ever worked so hard. It had been emotionally exhausting. Cute as Theo Swann was, his snake came back to mind, and she couldn't stop the shudder. She started the car and went home, thinking she should probably get back to the computer for a few hours and then press her dress for church in the morning. After arriving home, however, she made the mistake of sitting in the overstuffed chair to sort through her mail. Too comfortable to move, she read her mail and dozed for the next hour, the computer forgotten.

❧ ❧ ❧

Almost two weeks later, Nikki did a little dance as she watched the FedEx woman drive away. It always felt so satisfying to finish a book, especially if it was on time. She'd been asking the Lord to help her hold her focus for the last week, and by getting plenty of rest and keeping at it, she had gotten the job done. She now felt free to take a little time off, maybe a week or so. To start off, she decided to work in her yard. Winter would be upon her before she knew it, and although it was still warm, the air had the feeling of autumn. The trees were still holding their leaves, but the flowerbeds that had bloomed so lovely during midsummer were now dried out and ready to be cleared.

Nikki headed out to the garage for tools and started on the beds around the front door. She had a nice pile of debris in the wheelbarrow when she spotted the snake. For several seconds she was frozen with fear, but after a few moments of deep breathing, she slowly pushed off her knees and told herself to remain calm. She had no more hit the road, however, than she began to run. Tearing like a mad woman down the street, she shot onto the large porch of the huge white house and knocked as if her life depended on it.

The door wasn't long in opening, and Nikki began to thoughtlessly babble as soon as she saw the man inside.

"Are you my neighbor?" Her chest heaved in her fear.

"Yes, may I—" he began, but got no further.

"A snake! It's right by the house. I don't know what to do; I just wanted to clear the plants and there it was, not big, but a snake! I don't know what to do."

"Let me get Theo," the man managed to get in.

"What if it's poisonous?"

"We'll be careful."

Leaving the door open, the man moved back inside. Nikki's eyes went back to her house as if she could see the snake from there. Not two minutes passed before the man was back, both Theo and Petra with him.

"Hello, Nikki," Petra said as if they were headed to a parade.

"There's a snake" was all Nikki could say, her voice still breathless.

"Theo will get it," she responded with confidence, following her father and brother off the porch. The man strode out confidently, the children with him, but Nikki hung back a little. In fact, they had to stop and wait for her at the picket fence.

"Where is it?" the man asked.

"There," Nikki pointed. "To the left side of the porch."

Theo stepped forward, and it took all Nikki had not to stop him.

"Here it is, Dad. It looks like a garter snake."

"I think you're right." The man had gone up right behind him.

With a long pole that Nikki hadn't even noticed before, Theo touched it. Nothing happened, so he tried again. Under his father's watchful eyes, the little boy bent and lifted the snake in his hand. He carried it out toward Petra and Nikki. Nikki had to stop herself from stepping behind the little girl.

"It's dead," he said sadly.

"Oh." Nikki was surprised. She didn't know how she felt about that—a little sad because of Theo's face, but relieved for herself.

"Well, thank you for checking for me. I'm sorry to have disturbed you."

"Not at all," the man replied, and Nikki finally looked at him. "I'm Dorian Swann, by the way."

Nikki shook the large hand that was held out to her and introduced herself.

"Nikki Brinks."

"You're the writer."

"Yes," Nikki said, but her mind was wandering. "Did you say Dorian Swann?"

"Yes."

"Are you the doctor?"

"Yes."

Nikki nodded.

"Where have you heard the name?"

Nikki smiled. "When I first moved back, my mother wrote down all the emergency numbers to have by the phone; she listed yours as the doctor."

Dorian smiled. "When you say moved back, do you just mean to Pine Tree or to this house?"

"To this house. I grew up here."

"Then I could ask you who lived in my house?"

"Sure. There weren't that many families."

"We bought it from a man named Pike."

"I didn't know him," Nikki began but then looked down to see Theo calmly holding the dead snake. She started in a way no one could miss.

"I'll tell you what I want you to do, Theo," his father spoke up kindly. "Why don't you get the shovel and bury the snake in our backyard. Petra and I will stay here and help Nikki with her yard; you come back when you're through."

"All right."

"I'm sorry," Nikki murmured as soon as Theo was out of earshot. "For a moment I forgot about it, and then it was so close to me."

"That's fine, Nikki," Dorian assured her. "Theo would think nothing of it. The kids' babysitter doesn't like Brutus, so Theo has learned to be sensitive."

As soon as he said this, he turned to load a small pile of dead flowers into the wheelbarrow. He then picked up the rake and began to work around one of the bushes. Nikki went back to her knees, only a little bit watchful to see if the snake had a family.

"So which was the first family you remember living in our house?"

"That would be the Cavanaughs, Max and Eileen. They moved when I was about 10, maybe as old as 12. Then the house sat empty for about a year before Twitchells bought it. They were there until my last year of high school. I remember because their oldest daughter was crushed that we wouldn't be graduating together.

"The Wilkinsons bought it from the Twitchells, but then I went off to college, and my mother was ready for a change. She sold our house and moved to Maine. After that I can't tell you."

"Actually," Dorian said while he raked, "you filled in just about everyone. I know that Charles Brookwell built it in 1925, only lived in it a year, and then sold it to another family, but I couldn't find any record between them and Wilkinsons."

Wondering who else he'd asked, Nikki then wanted to know who lived at the end of the road now.

"A young couple," Dorian told her. "Their last name is Ross, and they tell me they don't know anyone around here."

"You need to have coffee with one of the old-timers in town to get filled in."

Dorian smiled. "I think you just called yourself old."

Nikki laughed. "Some days I feel it."

"It's all done," Theo proclaimed as he joined the group once again. "And we won't even tell Mrs. Butram, because she'd rather not know."

"Is Mrs. Butram your babysitter?" Nikki asked from her place on the ground.

"Well, she's more Petra's than mine, but she does the cooking and keeps the house clean. She's nice, but she doesn't like Brutus."

Nikki smiled in understanding, all the time thinking it didn't sound as if there was a mother in this household.

"We're having soup tonight," Petra told Nikki. The little girl was supposed to be putting little sticks in the wheelbarrow, but she was sitting on the porch steps staring at Nikki. "Do you want to have some with us?"

Nikki smiled at her but didn't answer. She pushed to her feet and put her load of leaves and vines with the others. It was getting fairly full, so she lifted the handles and started around the back of the house, but Dorian stopped her to reiterate Petra's question.

"We would like you to join us, Nikki."

Nikki looked at him and then at the children who were watching her in anticipation.

"Brutus is in a cage," Theo told her. "He can't get out."

Nikki's heart melted, but she still asked of Dorian, "Are you certain? I know you weren't planning on me."

"We have plenty."

Nikki met his eyes, and for a moment she couldn't look away. She had felt his gaze on her from time to time but hated to read something that wasn't there.

"I'd love to join you," she said softly. "I baked a loaf of bread in my breadmaker this morning. May I bring that?"

"That's fine," Dorian answered as he came to take the handles from her. "Where to?"

"The burning barrel behind the garage."

Nikki and the children followed, and all hands, large and small, helped empty everything into the can. They went back to the house as a group and finished the beds and bushes all the way around. Petra did more talking than working, but she was such a character that Nikki could only laugh.

"I want to see in your house," she said at one point.

"Petra Swann." Her father spoke softly but with a note the little girl did not miss.

"I'm sorry."

"That's all right, Petra. If your father says it's okay, you may."

Dorian shook his head. "We'll see it some other time, Petra. We need to finish up here and head home to start dinner."

"When are you coming, Nikki?" This came from Theo.

"When would you like me?"

"We usually eat at six o'clock."

"I'll come then, shall I?"

He nodded and smiled at her and left Nikki thinking what a special family they were.

"Thank you for all your help," she said to the doctor as they readied to leave.

"You're welcome. It looks as though you're in pretty good shape for when the leaves start to fall."

"Does everyone still rake and burn until we're sick of the smoke?"

"I'm afraid so," he said with a laugh. "We'll see you in a few hours, okay?"

"Yes. Is there anything else I can bring?"

"Just yourself," he said so softly that Nikki almost missed it. Again their eyes met, his very dark, almost black, and Nikki's a light green. The doctor smiled suddenly and said goodbye. Nikki stayed where she was for a moment and then moved into the house. She took a shower, washed her hair, and worked on some things that had been waiting while she finished the book, but through it all her neighbors were not very far from her mind.

❧ ❧ ❧

"You read my books, Theo?" Nikki asked several hours later as the children showed her their rooms.

"Oh, yes. They're some of my favorites."

"Theo," Nikki sat on the edge of his bed, "do you suppose you could do me a huge favor?"

"I think so."

"I just finished writing a book," Nikki explained. "If you could read it and tell me what you think, I could know if it's going to be a good story before it goes to print. Do you think your father would mind?"

"I don't think so, but I could ask him."

"That would be great. I would want you to give me your honest opinion."

"All right," he nodded congenially.

"You'll let me know what your father says?"

"Yes."

"Can you see my room now?"

Petra had come to the door, looking very much like a 5-year-old going on 15.

"Yes, I can," Nikki answered her and rose. "Thank you for showing me your room, Theo. It looks great."

"You're welcome."

Petra's room was adorable, with a Noah's ark theme that included a ceiling covered with clouds and wainscot paint that resembled the ocean filled with sea life. Nikki was captivated. Someone had gone to a lot of work, someone who painted very well.

"This is wonderful, Petra!"

"It's Noah's ark."

"I see that. I like it," Nikki told her, but the little girl just stared at her. It was so hard to know what she might be thinking. There was a keen intelligence in these children that Nikki found fascinating. They seemed very independent as well, but not distant or too grown up.

Theo wandered into his sister's room at that point and asked Nikki about the book she'd just written. They were in a discussion over it when Dorian came up to tell them that dinner was ready. He waited for the children and Nikki to precede him down the stairs, but Nikki held back.

"Dr. Swann," she began.

"Dorian," he said softly.

Nikki nodded but looked preoccupied as she whispered, "Where is Brutus?"

The doctor's voice was just as low. "In the basement."

Relief covered her face. "Thank you."

Dorian didn't say anything but only stared at her. Nikki felt self-conscious.

"You think I'm foolish, don't you?"

"Not in the least. Snakes are scary. I've never had a desire to have one, but Theo loves Brutus, and I can live with it."

Nikki smiled at him. He was doing a fine job. His children were sweet and respectful, and she saw signs all over the house that Christ was preeminent.

"Shall we go down?" Dorian asked.

"Of course." Nikki preceded him, and minutes later they all sat down to eat.

❧ ❧ ❧

A game of Junior Monopoly followed dinner and kitchen cleanup. Nikki couldn't remember when she'd had such a good time. The game very much followed the "luck" of the cards, and of all things, Petra won. She didn't seem overly boastful or surprised, and Theo informed Nikki that Petra won quite often.

As the children put the game away, Dorian made an announcement. "I'm going to walk Nikki to her door, and I want you guys to get ready for bed—pj's, teeth, everything. Once you've seen to all of that, you can wait for me in the living room."

The children bid Nikki goodnight and moved to obey their father. Petra even hugged Nikki before leaving the room. Dorian locked the front door as they left, and as soon as they hit the stairs, his guest spoke.

"You have wonderful children."

"I think so," Dorian said softly, "but then I'm biased."

"Well, I'm not, and I can assure you, they're very special."

"They like you too."

"Good. They really are welcome to visit whenever they like. If I'm in the middle of something, I'll be very honest about my time."

"Thank you. I'll make sure they know."

"Thank you for a wonderful evening and the help with the yard."

"You're welcome. We'll probably see you on Sunday."

"Yes," Nikki smiled warmly at him. "Goodnight, Dorian."

"Goodnight, Nikki."

Nikki let herself in the door, waving just before she shut and locked it. Dorian made his way home to put his children to bed. Nikki settled down with a book. Both were still wishing they'd had more time to get to know one another.

❧ ❧ ❧

"Hey, buddy, what are you doing up?"

It was much later that night, long past time for Theo to be asleep, but he was downstairs looking for his father, who was reading in the living room.

"I can't sleep."

Since this was totally unlike Theo, Dorian set his book aside. Theo climbed into his lap, and Dorian wrapped his arms around his son.

"What's up?"

"I can't stop thinking about Nikki."

Dorian looked down at the young image of his own face.

"I don't think she's the type to leave, Dad," the little boy said. "I don't think she would ever leave."

Dorian lay his forehead against Theo's and sighed.

Would this little boy ever forget the way his mother had left them? Would he ever look at other women and not compare them to Crystal Swann, who wanted out of motherhood so badly that she couldn't get away fast enough?

"I think maybe you're a little ahead of the game, Theo," Dorian said gently. "I just met Nikki today."

"I know, but she's the first one you've ever asked to dinner. Usually Petra gets in trouble for doing that, and today you let her."

"Nikki is our neighbor, Theo."

Theo's look was old beyond his years. Dorian wouldn't have been surprised if he'd laughed in disbelief, but he only looked at his father in skepticism.

"I like Nikki," Dorian said gently, "but that's all I'm willing to say on the subject, okay?"

"Okay." Theo's dark head nodded. "I just wanted to make sure you noticed how nice she was and that she seemed to like us too."

Dorian pressed a kiss to Theo's temple and held him close. "Thank you, Theo. Do you think you can sleep now?"

"Yeah. I think so."

Dorian carried his precious son to bed and decided to retire himself. He had to work the next day, but even telling himself that didn't help. It was very late before sleep came.

🦢 🦢 🦢

"Well, now, Michelle," Dorian said to the 11-year-old who was waiting for him in one of the exam rooms. "How is the ankle?"

"It feels pretty good. I hope the cast can come off."

Dorian moved toward the X rays which were clipped on light boxes mounted on the wall. "We'll just have a look and see. Your mom's not with you today?"

"She is, but there was some insurance paper she had to fill out. She said she'd be in as soon as she was done."

"This looks good," Dorian spoke as he studied the film. "See, here's the old X ray and here's today's. I think that cast can come off." The doctor turned with a smile when he said this, and that's when he spotted the book in Michelle's hand.

"You're reading a Dominique Brinks."

"Yeah." Michelle's eyes lit up. "She came to speak to our class last week."

"Theo told me."

"She even signed this for me." Michelle displayed the signature with pride. "And Theo's reading one of her books, one that hasn't even been published yet. Isn't that cool?"

"Yes, it is."

"He thinks it's her best yet."

Dorian smiled and turned to the door when Michelle's mother came in. The next 20 minutes were spent finishing up the appointment, and Dorian was glad it was not more complicated. He was having a hard time concentrating.

❧ ❧ ❧

"I brought my horse to show you." Petra began the conversation from Nikki's front step. She didn't bother with a greeting but picked things up just where she and Nikki had left off two days before.

"Oh, Petra, I'm so glad. It's a wonderful horse." Nikki croaked these words out, her head pounding. "But I have a terrible cold, so I don't think you should come in."

"Oh, all right. I'll come back tomorrow."

She left without saying another word, and Nikki felt too awful to say anything about a visit the next day. Still trying to convince herself that it wasn't that bad, Nikki went back to the living room sofa. She should have been in bed, but that would have been admitting defeat. Crawling beneath the quilt, she closed her eyes and prayed that her mother would drop in for another surprise visit.

❧ ❧ ❧

"What are we going to get Theo for his birthday?" Petra wanted to know that night at the supper table.

"I don't know. Have you asked Theo?"

"We can't do that," she said with five-year-old logic. "Then he'll know."

That Theo was sitting at the table with them did not seem to occur to Petra.

"Well, Pet, since Theo's birthday is at the end of November, I think we have a little bit of time."

"Can we invite Nikki to the party?"

"I don't know. And in truth, it's up to Theo if Nikki comes. Like I said, Petra, we have time to decide."

"I think it would be fun if Nikki came," Theo put in in his sensible manner.

"She can't." Petra could change tracks faster than anyone could keep up.

"Why?" her brother wished to know.

"She has a cold."

Dorian was suddenly all ears, but his voice was as calm as always. "When did you see her, Petra?"

"Today. She liked my horse, but she said I shouldn't come in."

Dorian finished his meal in silence, but he was already making plans. It was Petra's night to help with dishes, but she was painfully slow, so Dorian did most of them. He then told the children to get their coats on. He slipped a can of chicken soup into his medical bag and led the way down the street.

For a time no one answered the door, and the young doctor realized he'd taken a five-year-old's word about Nikki's being sick. He was just about to check the garage for her car when he heard the turn of the deadbolt.

"Dorian," Nikki managed in a surprised croak.

"Petra said you were ill."

"Just a cold."

Dorian looked at her. Knowing some of the different bugs that were being passed around the schools, he strongly suspected that this was more than a cold. "May we come in?"

"Of course; I just didn't want you to catch anything."

"You probably caught this from one of the children at school, which probably means that we are already immune to it," Dorian said as he came in the door.

Nikki, who was cold all over again, went back to the sofa and was followed by her visitors. She sat down and watched as Dorian sat opposite her on the oak coffee table. Having been in the house several times, the children knew the way and wandered off to see her office full of cartoons.

"Here you go." Dorian handed her a thermometer. He waited until she'd stuck it in her mouth and then reached for her wrist. Blood pressure was next, and then it was time to consult the thermometer.

"Over 102°," he murmured softly before his hands went up to check the glands in her throat. "Headache?"

"Yes, and so cold. About an hour ago my ear started to hurt."

Dorian stared at her and said softly, "I don't suppose you thought to call me."

"I knew you'd be out of the office by now."

"I live up the street," he reminded her in a low voice.

"I think you must have better things to do than pay house calls to pesky neighbors."

Again Dorian only stared at her before saying, "You couldn't be more wrong."

Nikki closed her eyes. "Please don't scold me, Dorian. I feel awful."

"I'm sorry," he said softly. "Let's have a look at those ears."

While this exam was underway, Petra wandered back in and sat close to the writer.

"Does it hurt, Nikki?"

"Yes, Petra," she answered with her eyes closed.

"My dad will fix you."

Nikki managed a small smile.

"Both of your ears are infected," Dorian sat back and stated.

"Both?"

"Yes, the right is worse than the left." He was reaching into his bag. "Are you allergic to any medications, Nikki?"

"No."

Dorian took something from the bag. "I want you to take one of these now and one before bed. It's amoxicillin. There's enough in this envelope for morning and noon tomorrow, and when I come home I'll bring the rest of your prescription." Dorian stood. "I'll get you some water."

Nikki shut her eyes until he returned and then obediently swallowed the pill he gave her.

"Have you had anything to eat today?" the doctor wanted to know.

Nikki looked at him. "I had some yogurt, but I couldn't taste it, so I gave up."

"I brought a can of soup. The kids and I will heat it for you."

Nikki thanked him and watched him walk from the room. It took her a moment to realize that Petra was still with her, those dark eyes watching her with concern.

"Do you feel better now, Nikki? Did the medicine help?"

"Not yet, Petra, but I'm sure it will."

The little girl nodded and put her hand on Nikki's arm. If Nikki had felt more like herself, she'd have taken her hand. Not long afterward, Theo and Dorian came with a mug of soup and a large glass of apple juice. They sat with Nikki while she ate most of the soup and then rose to put their coats back on. Dorian wrote something on a piece of paper and left it on the table.

"This is our home phone. If you need anything or start to feel worse, call me, even if you just want to talk about your symptoms."

Nikki nodded. "Thank you."

Dorian watched her, hating to leave but knowing he had no choice. "I'll be back tomorrow as soon as I can get away, no later than about six o'clock."

"Okay."

Nikki stood long enough to be certain the doors were all locked and then gave up. A double ear infection! It was time to admit she was sick and go to bed.

※ ※ ※

Nikki didn't feel much better in the morning, but late as it was, almost eleven o'clock, she still made herself get up, shower, and dress. Refusing to return to bed, she headed for the living room sofa and put in a video. Nikki was usually strict with herself about watching Christmas movies out of season—the holidays were more special if she saved them until at least Thanksgiving—but today she was in need of a dose of *White Christmas*. She kept the sound very low and dozed off before the movie ended. She woke to someone knocking at the door. It was Mrs. Butram; Petra was behind her.

"Hello, Nikki," she spoke kindly, her arms full. "Petra and I have brought you a little something to eat."

"Oh, Mrs. Butram, how nice."

Nikki held the door open wide and tried to stay on her feet. The stuffiness of her ears made her feel as if the room were spinning.

"Go back to your seat, Nikki," the older woman ordered, sizing up the situation. "We'll take this to the kitchen and then bring you a nice hot bowl of soup."

Nikki thought she smelled food, but she couldn't be certain; her head felt as though it was stuffed with cotton. She sat back down on the living room sofa, and a few moments later Mrs. Butram materialized carrying a tray which held a mug of soup, some tiny muffins, and hot tea.

"Oh, my," Nikki croaked. "How nice."

"This is my mother's recipe for colds," the older woman informed her. "She swears by it."

"It looks wonderful," Nikki said as she took a sip. She looked up in surprise. "I can taste it."

"That's the dill. Now you drink as much as you can and rest all day today. By tomorrow you'll be feeling much more the thing."

Nikki smiled at her and then looked down at Petra, who had drawn close.

"My dad is bringing you medicine."

"Yes. Isn't that nice of him?"

Petra nodded. "He'll fix you."

The adults in the room shared a smile.

"Adores him, this one does," Mrs. Butram said softly, and Nikki's eyes went back to the little girl who was still watching her in concern. When she felt better she would have to plan a tea party or something equally fun just for the two of them.

The visitors weren't long in staying, but Nikki thought about their visit for a long time. "Adores him" had been the babysitter/housekeeper's words. The writer's mind went back to the Swanns' visit the night before and how kind the doctor had been. Without much effort, Nikki found it very easy to believe that Petra adored her father.

🌹 🌹 🌹

One week later Nikki knocked on the Swanns' door and waited. It didn't take long for the young man of the household to answer.

"Hi, Theo, you're just the person I want to see. Do you have time to talk about the book?"

"Sure. Come on in."

Nikki stepped in the door, notepad in hand. The whole house smelled as if Mrs. Butram had been baking. Nikki followed Theo into the living room and sat when he did. She could see Petra coloring at the kitchen table, but other than a brief wave, she seemed unaware of the two in the living room.

"Should I tell Mrs. Butram that I'm here, Theo?"

"She's already left."

"Your dad then?"

"He's not home just yet. A few days a week we have time in between."

"Oh, all right. Should I come back when your dad gets home?"

"No, this is fine. I can't open the door to just anyone, but we know you."

"Okay," Nikki nodded, taking it all in. Feeling protective all of a sudden, she had to remind herself that she'd come on business. "Did you have a chance to finish the book, Theo?"

"Yes, and—"

"Theo," Nikki cut him off. "I want to say something before you do, okay?"

The little boy nodded.

"Just because I'm your neighbor—just because you know me—doesn't mean you have to be easy on me. I want you to give your honest opinion. If you like some of the book, none of the book, or all of the book, I want you to tell me. If there were certain points that confused you, or were not well-written, you need to tell me. Don't worry about my having hurt feelings or being upset. I won't be. Okay?"

"Okay." Theo would have gone on, but Nikki opened her pad and poised her pen.

"Are you going to take notes?" he asked.

"Yes. That way I can remember the changes I need to make."

Theo nodded but then said very honestly, "I liked it. I especially liked Brad. He was cool and really brave."

Nikki nodded, feeling very pleased.

"And what about the whole mystery—was it believable? Do you think it could have really happened?"

Before he could answer, a door opened somewhere in the kitchen, and Petra's voice could be heard greeting her father. A sudden flush coming to her face, Nikki stood. By the time Dorian made the front room, she looked ready to bolt.

"Well, hello," he said kindly, and Nikki felt her face grow very red.

"I'm sorry to intrude. You must be ready to eat dinner. I'll come back later."

Dorian watched her for a moment and then looked to his son.

"We're talking about the book," Theo explained.

"Great." Dorian sat down as if he had all the time in the world. "I'm eager to hear all of Theo's comments too."

Nikki slowly sat back down, her face still hot. She studied the notepad in front of her as though she'd written down the secrets of life and worked to gather her composure.

"You were asking me if I thought the mystery was real?"

"That's right." Nikki looked up and smiled gratefully. "Thank you, Theo. What did you think?"

"It was very real, but I didn't understand how Brad got out of the cave."

Nikki made a wry face. "I wondered about that when I wrote it." The writer's face became thoughtful. "Did you understand the cave had a rear entrance?"

"No," Theo's brows rose. "I don't remember that."

Nikki's shake of the head was directed at herself. "That's because I didn't do a good job explaining the layout."

"Where was that part?"

"Do you have the manuscript handy?"

"In my room, I'll get it."

Theo ran up the stairs that led up from the front door, and Nikki looked over to find Dorian smiling at her. For some reason the smile reminded her of the paper in her pocket.

"I didn't think I would see you," she said as she reached for the blank check. "I signed this and left you a note asking you to fill in the amount. But now I'll just give it to you."

Nikki stood, took a few steps across the room and held the check out to him, but Dorian only stared at it.

"What is it for?"

"The medicine."

He dismissed it with a hand. "Don't worry about it."

"Are you sure? I don't want you to have to take care of it."

Dorian only shook his head as Theo came back into the room.

"Here it is," the little boy said.

Nikki stuffed the check back into her pocket, turned, and took the stack of papers from Theo's hands. She found the place they needed, and with heads bent together, they studied the chapter for the next ten minutes. Nikki made notes in the margin of the page, seeming pleased with the changes.

"Anything else?"

Theo shook his head. "I don't think so. It was a good book, Nikki. Maybe even my favorite."

Nikki sighed. "I can't tell you what a help you've been, Theo."

"Why was it such a help?"

"Because you're the right age for this book. My editor reads it, and different people at the publishing house read it, but I don't have any kids who can look it over and give me their feedback. Kids read my books, so input from someone your age is the most valuable thing to me."

Theo smiled. She had a way of making him feel so good. And he had liked the book. It was a great story. It had been so cool the way she'd told his whole class that he'd agreed to read it for her. He'd been a little bit embarrassed, but when everyone found out Dominique Brinks was his neighbor and thought that was cool, his embarrassment faded. And besides that, she was just Nikki: not a writer, but a neighbor who was really nice and seemed just right for his dad.

"I'd like to take you to lunch some time, Theo," Nikki said as she stood. "We'll set a date one of these days and go to Camden's for sandwiches and ice cream. Would you like that?"

"Yeah!"

"Great. That will be my thanks to you. We'll do it real soon."

Theo's smile was infectious, and Nikki thought if she knew him better, she'd have given him a hug.

"I'd better go," she said with a smile that encompassed both the older and younger Swann without having to look directly at Dorian. "Thanks again, Theo, and thank you again, Dorian, for the medicine. I'll see you later."

They both saw her to the door, and as before, Nikki was very aware of the doctor's eyes on her. She couldn't help but wonder what he was thinking but knew there was no way to find out. She speculated on it all the way through her own evening meal and even as she readied for bed. She had just picked up the book she was reading when the phone rang.

"Did I call too late?" Dorian's voice sounded in her ear, and Nikki had to breathe deeply at the pleasure that ran through her.

"No, not at all. I was going to read for a while."

"I wanted to thank you for what you said to Theo. You can't believe how excited he was that you valued his opinion."

"It's I who owe the thanks, Dorian. He was a huge help. When the galleys come, I can make the changes or even fax them in ahead of time."

"The galleys are what you proof before the book goes to print, right?"

"Yes. I should have them in a few weeks."

"When does this book come out?"

"January."

"And the cover, do you work on that as well?"

"I have input, but artwork is not my strong point, so I leave a lot of that up to my publisher."

Before they knew it, an hour had passed, the conversation ranging far. Dorian told her about the book he was reading to the kids before they went to bed each night, and for some reason that led to the way his hours worked and who his partners were. Nikki had questions about his hospital and clinic work, and he asked her about her family and more about the way she got started as a writer. It was after 10:30 before they hung up, but it was as if they never left off. Waiting at

night until the kids were in bed and things were settled, Dorian called six times in the next ten days.

❧ ❧ ❧

The end of October brought cold weather and lots
of sunshine. The days were shorter, but Nikki was still
accomplishing much. She had been writing steadily
since she recovered from her ear infections, and she
knew it was time for a day off. She planned to spend it
in the kitchen, baking, putting together her menu for
November, writing letters, and catching up on small,
fun jobs. She knew it would be a nice change from her
desk work, especially with no deadline breathing down
her neck.

The baking was first, and Nikki saw very soon that
she would need a trip to the grocery store in town.
Making a quick list, she checked her purse for keys and
wallet, and walked to the garage. She moved down the
street, her mind already wandering the aisles of
Patron's Market. She was almost to the Swann home
before she spotted Petra playing in the street. Nikki
stopped the car and rolled the passenger window
down.

"Petra," Nikki called to her and waited for her to
approach. Nikki's small car put their faces on a closer
level.

"Hi, Nikki."

"Hi, Petra. I wonder if maybe you shouldn't play in
the street."

"Why not?" she asked sincerely, and as usual, Nikki
had to smile; Petra had that effect on her.

"You might get hit by a car."

Petra's confused brow relaxed. "That's all right; my dad's a doctor."

She had Nikki this time. There wasn't a thing she could find to say. The blonde writer just stared down at Petra's adorable, confident little face and found herself speechless.

"Are you going to town, Nikki?"

"Yes," the older female answered absently. "I've got to go to the grocery store."

"I'm playing."

Nikki nodded, still trying to recover. "Well, have a good time."

"Thank you," Petra said and skipped off on her merry way. Nikki drove on, a small shake to her head. Petra's logic was probably normal for a five-year-old, but Nikki had little contact with children, so she found the little girl quite amusing. She chuckled to herself as she completed her list and even knew what she would say to Petra if she saw her again, but the little girl was out of sight when Nikki returned home.

❧   ❧   ❧

Nikki paced next to the phone in her kitchen and told herself she shouldn't. Stopping many times to stare at it, she even reached for it one time but pulled her hand back.

Just because he's called a few times doesn't mean he wants you calling him. Maybe he's having a hard time putting the kids down. You can presume, Nikki, and you know that. But the talk didn't do much for her heart. She still desperately wanted to call Dorian Swann and tell him about her brief conversation with Petra. He was sure to think it was fun. Nikki had just about given up when the phone rang. She took a deep breath, reminding herself it could be anyone, and lifted the receiver.

"How was your day?" It was the way he always started, and Nikki's smile, had he but seen it, was huge.

"Great. I was hoping you would call."

"You were?" He sounded very pleased.

"Yes. I spoke with your daughter this morning and got the quote of the day."

"What did she say?" She could hear the smile in his voice.

Nikki filled him in and smiled when she heard him laugh on the other end; it was a hushed laugh and she knew the kids must be settled in bed.

"She's so funny, Dorian, and she doesn't even try."

"You're certainly right about that. She's decided that you need a pet, by the way, so the discussion around the table tonight was all about that."

"What pet did she decide on?"

"I think the last one under consideration was a white rat."

Nikki made a noise that told Dorian she was shuddering, and he laughed all over again.

"I don't suppose you want to come down to the porch and visit for a while," he said suddenly, his voice soft and inviting. It was the first time he'd ever asked her to do more than speak on the phone.

It was Nikki's turn to chuckle. "I don't have that many coats."

"You could wear your snowmobile suit."

"I don't have a snowmobile suit."

"Are you serious?"

"Yes. I've never needed one."

"Well, you do now. We have two sleds, and we'll have snow before you know it."

"Sounds fun."

"It is fun, so you better get the proper clothing."

Nikki knew an invitation when she heard it, and again her smile was huge and her heart felt as light as a balloon. As with the other nights, they talked for at least an hour. She had never had a relationship like this. When she saw Dorian at church or on the street, she felt shy and a little tongue-tied, but on the phone they were able to talk about anything. She already knew that he was a wonderful man, and the way he loved his children was causing Nikki to fall in love with him.

Dorian's feelings were on the same path. After he hung up the phone, he sat for a long time and thought about his neighbor. He'd not been searching for another wife, but right now he would be lying to himself if he didn't admit that Nikki certainly seemed to fit the bill. She was so special, so full of life and caring. Lately he was having a hard time keeping his mind on anything but her. He finally took himself off to bed, but he fell asleep as he always did when they talked, their conversation still going through his mind.

❧ ❧ ❧

Halloween fell on a Tuesday. Although Nikki had seen advertisements for candy in the market's newspaper ad, the day almost passed before she remembered what day it was. Living on such a quiet, dead-end street on the outskirts of town gave her little reason to plan. However, there were still Theo and Petra. She could not and would not want to forget them.

It was coming onto four o'clock when she put together a plate of cookies and headed down the street. Darkness was falling fast. The days were shorter now, and the very air smelled of winter. Nikki's mittened hand knocked on the door, and even though she could see lights inside, she had to knock a second time before the door was answered.

"Hi, Theo," Nikki began enthusiastically but cut off when she saw his face. "Everything okay?"

"No," he said softly.

"Can I do anything?"

The little boy shrugged, looking miserable. Nikki peeked around the door and saw the cause of the problem. Petra was standing in the middle of the coffee table, her costume on but not in place. Obviously a hand-me-down of some sort, it hung from one shoulder and drooped at the waist. The little girl in question was just barely holding her tears.

"May I come in, Theo?"

He nodded and stepped back, closing the door behind her.

Nikki slipped the cookie plate onto the first available surface and approached the little girl. Huge tears seemed to do the impossible as they filled Petra's lower lids but did not spill. Her chin quivered uncontrollably.

"Well, now." Nikki's voice was gentle. "It looks as if you could use a pin here and there."

Petra made no reply.

"Mrs. Butram gone already?" Nikki asked, but the little girl remained mute. Nikki looked behind her to see Theo nod. It was only then that she realized he was already in his own costume; she thought he might be Zorro or Robin Hood but was afraid to ask. She turned back to the little girl. Dilapidated as the costume was, Nikki was quite certain she was supposed to be a princess.

"I think what we need here are a few tucks." Nikki's voice became suddenly businesslike. She glanced down to see a sewing basket lying on the sofa and began to go through it. She found thread and needle and a few large pins.

Nikki gently turned Petra until her back was to her and began to gather the excess material. It wouldn't look all that great in the back, but at least the front would fit. Nikki was vaguely aware of Theo taking a chair to watch, but she said nothing to either child until she turned Petra to the front again and began working on the waist.

"I was a princess one year for Halloween," Nikki mentioned conversationally, her eyes still on her hands. "I decided to do my own costume and made a horrible mess of it. My mother had offered to help, but I wanted to do it. When it was all over, she ended up making me a beautiful costume, but when I smiled and danced around in delight because I thought I looked so pretty, she reminded me that the costume didn't tell anyone what I was like inside.

"She reminded me of the verse that tells us that people look at the outside but God looks on the heart. I needed to hear that. I had been so angry about my costume and not at all nice to my mother when she first tried to help, and I knew that even though I looked like a princess on Halloween night, my heart was black with selfishness and sin."

For the first time Nikki let her eyes meet Petra's. That little girl was watching her intently as Nikki knew she had been the whole time.

"Do you understand what I'm talking about, Petra?"

The little girl nodded. "I was angry at Theo."

"Were you?"

"Yes. I need to tell him I'm sorry."

Nikki smiled at her and drew her tenderly into her arms. Petra hugged her in return.

Watching them from the kitchen, Dorian felt his throat close. *I never dreamed of the way You would provide, Lord. Never in my wildest imaginations would I have thought someone like Nikki Brinks would move next door. I don't know what You have for us, Father, but I pray that You'll show us. She's so special, and the children care for her already.*

Dorian stopped when he realized Nikki was staring at him. He let his eyes hold hers but fought the urge to cross the room and take her in his arms as she'd done with Petra.

"Your father's here," he saw more than heard her say. The children went to him, and Nikki held her place. She watched him bend over and hug them and then speak quietly for their ears alone. Theo moved deeper into the kitchen then, but Petra came back to the living room.

"Thank you, Nikki," she said as soon as she stopped in front of her.

"You're welcome, Petra. You look very nice."

"I have to talk to Theo now."

"All right."

While Nikki watched Petra go, Dorian took the princess' place. He stood very close and looked down into Nikki's eyes.

"Thank you," he murmured softly.

Nikki's smile was warm as she looked up at him.

"Come with us tonight," he urged, his voice low. "We're going into town for a little while to trick-or-treat. Please come."

"All right."

"We'll pick you up in about an hour, unless you want to eat with us."

"I have something in the oven at home, but I'll be ready when you come."

Another few seconds passed before either of them moved.

"I'd better go," Nikki said with obvious reluctance.

"Okay." Dorian walked her to the door and thanked her one more time. Nikki could only assure him that the pleasure had been hers. The doctor eventually went back to the children, and Nikki walked back up the street to ready for trick-or-treating. The cookies, her reason for her visit in the first place, were completely forgotten.

❧ ❧ ❧

Four days later on Saturday evening, Nikki got into the front seat of Dorian's car and greeted the children in the back, much as she had Halloween night. They'd covered some 30 homes on Halloween, treat bags in hand, and afterward Dorian had asked Nikki to go out with him on the weekend. She had gladly accepted. What she hadn't expected was that the children would be joining them. She didn't comment, however, and indeed, felt very much like laughing. She had dressed in her best, taking great pains with her hair, makeup, and nails—all, she assumed, to spend the evening in a family restaurant. She wasn't put off, only amused at herself and a bit confused. She was even more so when Dorian went the four miles into town only to turn up the street into a residential neighborhood.

"We're staying overnight with Mrs. Butram," Petra informed her when the car glided smoothly to the curb.

"You are? How nice," Nikki turned and smiled. "Have you stayed here before?"

"A few times," Theo filled in. "She has a nice dog, and Mr. Butram plays games with us."

"I hope you have a great time."

"Bye, Nikki," Petra called, climbing from the back. Theo waved, and Nikki kept her seat until Dorian returned. He turned to her the moment he slipped behind the wheel, a wide smile on his face.

"You thought the kids were joining us, didn't you?"

Nikki laughed. "Yes. I thought I'd misunderstood you and dressed all wrong."

His smile was still in place as he put the car into gear and moved down the road. They didn't say much as he drove almost 20 miles to a restaurant in Montpelier, but as soon as they sat down across from each other, the words just flowed.

"How was your day?" he asked.

"Busy, but good. I feel as though I got a lot done. How about yours?"

"It started with a birth. I delivered twins at 5:30 this morning," Dorian announced with a smile.

"Twins." Nikki's voice dropped with wonder. "How are all three of them doing?"

"Just great. It's a first delivery, so everything was new and special."

"Two boys . . . ?" Nikki prompted.

"A boy and a girl, both dark-haired and howling with great health."

"That's wonderful, but you must be tired."

"I *was* tired. I was tired when Petra decided she needed every stuffed animal she owned with her at the Butrams' tonight, and also when Theo said he'd forgotten to feed Brutus, but as soon as I saw you in that dress, the fatigue suddenly lifted."

Nikki smiled at the compliment, thinking Dorian looked wonderful too. His suit was a medium shade of navy and his shirt a bright white. The tie at his throat was a subtle red and blue stripe that only accentuated his aquiline features, still brown from the summer.

"You're Greek, aren't you, Dorian?" Nikki asked suddenly.

He eyed her in speculation. "What was the giveaway, my nose or the black hair and eyes?"

"Your name and the children's names were the first things I noticed."

Dorian nodded. "My mother is Greek, and when I was first married, my wife loved my Greek name and the idea of naming our first son Theodore." He hadn't planned to talk about Crystal, but it seemed the right time to add, "but that, along with everything else in our marriage, soon lost all appeal for her."

"Where is she, Dorian?" Nikki asked gently.

"I don't know right now," he admitted. "In the last five years, I've seen her only twice: the day she left the children and me and the day she showed up with her lawyer, asking me to sign divorce papers."

Nikki felt a sting behind her eyes just at the thought of what he'd gone through. Her look was compassionate, but she stayed quiet so the man across from her could share.

"She never wanted to move to Vermont, but I didn't know that until we'd been here a year. I knew everything was not fine, but most of the time she wouldn't talk to me. Now I'm able to see so many things I could have done better, but at the time I plodded along the best I could. For a while she agreed to meet with our pastor every week. I thought we were making headway, but then she found out she was pregnant with Petra, and you'd have thought I asked her to give up her life. She was inconsolable. She stopped taking care of Theo, and I feared that she would take her own life or even the baby's.

"Petra wasn't 48 hours old when I came to the hospital and found Crystal dressed and ready to leave. There was no talking to her. She called a cab and left, not even returning home for her things. I took my baby daughter home alone, and Theo and I picked out her name. I nearly lost my practice in the year after that, trying to take care of the kids and see to my patients at the same time. Then when Petra was two, Crystal showed up and wanted to see me. She came to the office so the kids weren't there, and since I'd been given two years to think about it, I knew what I would do.

"I asked her if she was willing to work on the marriage. I told her I loved her and still wanted us to share our lives. She wanted none of it. I questioned her several times—several different ways. I had to be sure. When I was positive it was over in her heart, I signed the papers.

"I'll never forget that day. I don't know how I finished my rounds; it had to have been the Lord. I made myself tell Theo that evening at bedtime, and although he cried a little, he was very brave. I wasn't brave at all. I cried the entire evening and again when I talked to Pastor Andersen.

"But all was not black," he shared softly. "I grew more spiritually that year than I had my whole life. I was forced to lean on the Lord and be in His Word in a way I never had before. I know that God works all things together for good for those who love God and are called according to His purpose, and He's been the One to help me move on. I feel no anger or bitterness, only a deep desire to be there for my kids and show them a better way."

"Thank you for telling me, Dorian."

"It's important that you know, Nikki," he told her seriously, his eyes on hers. "Don't misunderstand what I'm about to say next, but there were things that Crystal never told me. It can't be that way between husband and wife or two people who are thinking about marriage."

"I quite agree with you," Nikki said, not put off at all. "I have a friend in New York who told me she'd met the man of her dreams, but he wasn't ready to have her meet his family or to talk about his past. Yet she was sure he was the one. I told her outright that she could be walking into a world of hurt. I'm thankful that her family felt the same way and that she listened to us. She's still getting to know him, but there's been no more talk of marriage."

"You were a good friend to tell her the truth."

Nikki nodded. "I'm still trying to figure out how good of a friend you are," Nikki suddenly said with a teasing glint in her eye.

"How's that?"

"Well, you've asked me to dinner but waved the waiter on three times. I'm starving, Dorian."

He smiled. "I knew you were going to be opinionated."

Nikki chuckled. "I'm taking lessons from your daughter."

Dorian found this highly amusing but still got the point. Their dinner orders were given and their salads delivered just a short time later. It was a fabulous evening. They dined and talked until very late and then slowly drove back to the street where they lived. Once outside Nikki's house, they sat in the car and talked for two more hours. They both knew it was going to be tough to get up in the morning for church, but both agreed it would be worth it.

Thanksgiving, Christmas, and New Year's came and went, and in those weeks Nikki and Dorian talked on the phone or saw each other nearly every day. Nikki flew to be with Tim and her mother for Christmas, but they drove her back and were able to meet Dorian and the children. Both were very impressed with the family and could see for themselves what Nikki had written in letters: Nikki and Dorian were very much in love. Dorian's family was scheduled to visit at the end of January, and all were looking forward to it. But before that time, there was a lot of Vermont winter to be enjoyed.

It was during this time, a snowy day about the middle of that month, that Dorian, Nikki, and the kids ventured out on the snowmobiles. They had gone two other times during the season, but now there was more snow. Nikki rode behind Theo, and Petra held on tightly to the back of Dorian on the first sled. Nikki loved it, feeling that she could go for miles. For her, the time to head back and warm up by the fire in the Swanns' living room came all too soon. But Petra's cold little hands gave them no choice.

Back at the house, the fire and hot chocolate were just what was needed, and the kids even volunteered to see to the microwave popcorn. While they were out of the room, Dorian picked up Nikki's hand and kissed the back before entwining their fingers.

"Pastor asked me a question this morning."

Nikki took her gaze from their hands, his so dark and hers so fair, to look at him. "About?"

"Us."

She studied Dorian's eyes for a moment. They were normally so expressive, compassionate, and kind in the extreme, but right now she couldn't tell what he was thinking.

"What exactly did he ask you?"

"He wanted to know if we would be joining the marriage class soon."

"And what did you tell him?"

"I said I would have to ask you."

Nikki's heart beat against her ribs until she thought they would break, but excited as she was, one thing was holding her back. She glanced over her shoulder to see if the kids were ready to join them, but they were still occupied. Her eyes went back to Dorian, a worried frown creasing her brow. She opened her mouth to speak, but the doctor cut in.

"Did I mention to you that Theo gave his snake away?"

Nikki blinked. "No," she said softly.

"He did." Dorian's voice was conversational, but his eyes kept track of Nikki's every move. "There was a boy in his class who really wanted it, and Theo felt it would be best. We delivered it yesterday."

"Is Theo upset?"

"Not at all." Dorian replied kindly. "He knew you would never be comfortable with it. And as much as he likes Brutus, he likes you more."

Nikki couldn't help throwing her arms around his neck. Dorian's own arms came up to hold her tight, and Nikki squeezed him as if she would never let go. They were still hugging when the kids joined them.

"Is Nikki all right?" Petra wanted to know.

"Yes, she's just happy."

Nikki shifted back to the room then and found Theo with her eyes. She had not cried but still felt as though she could. She waved Theo toward her with a hand and spoke when he sat by her side.

"Are you sad about Brutus?"

"No, not really. I can visit him at Richie's anytime I want. His mom said so."

Nikki's hand brushed the black curls from his forehead. "Have I told you that I love you, Theo?"

The sweet 11-year-old nodded and smiled.

"You love me too," Petra came close to remind Nikki.

"Yes, I do," Nikki said and pulled her into her lap. With an arm around Theo, the three snuggled together for a few minutes. It didn't last long because Petra felt it was her duty to hand out the popcorn, and after all, she told them, it was getting cold. Once Dorian and Nikki both had their bowls, the kids went to select a video, giving the adults a few moments alone. For a moment all Nikki could do was stare at the man beside her.

"I wasn't looking for love," she finally whispered, "but then there you were."

Dorian smiled and pressed a soft kiss to her lips. "Do you know when I fell in love with you?"

"No."

"At the pet show."

Nikki's eyes rounded. "The pet show? I didn't even see you."

"I know you didn't. You were too busy smiling at my daughter and trying not to show how terrified you were of Brutus." Dorian's eyes lovingly searched her face. "I would have said I was too busy even to think about marriage, but that was before I met the girl next door."

Nikki's smile was huge as she leaned toward him for another kiss.

"I guess this means I should tell Pastor we'll be in the class?" he asked, a teasing light in his eyes.

"Yes, please." Nikki's voice was fervent. "The sooner the better."

The kids chose that moment to return with a video, one that they'd seen many times. They sat on and between Dorian and Nikki, but Dorian still managed to have an arm along the back of the sofa, his hand on Nikki's shoulder.

Nikki watched the video, but her heart was elsewhere. *I'm going to be married, Lord. Isn't that wonderful? Please tell my dad, Lord. Tell him I've found someone as wonderful as he was to Mom and as wonderful as Tim is now.* Nikki could have prayed on for hours, but at that moment she caught Dorian's eyes on her.

"Are you all right?" he asked softly.

"Yes," Nikki whispered back, "just sending a message to my dad."

Dorian reached for her hand then and held it very tightly, his eyes glued to her face. Nikki was just as taken with him. Indeed, it was a good thing the kids didn't question them about the story, since neither one saw much more of the video that evening.

❧ ❧ ❧

The wedding was set for the first Saturday in June. It was warm and breezy, the weather almost as lovely as the bride herself. A small service was planned at the church with a large reception to follow at the community hall. Tim Warburton, who would walk Nikki down the aisle, Dorian, and Theo, who would stand as best man, went ahead to the church. The bride, her mother, and Petra, Nikki's maid of honor, were coming on their own.

"All right." Virginia's voice was all business. "Have we got everything?"

"I think so," Nikki said, her eyes glancing about. "Petra, did you use the bathroom?"

"Yes, and I washed my hands."

"Good job. Let's head to the car."

The three trooped out in all of their finery, Petra in pink lace, Virginia in pale blue silk, and Nikki in an old-fashioned white lace dress that fell to midcalf and showed off her high-buttoned white boots. The dress was not the type that needed much babying, so she climbed behind the wheel of her small car and they headed down the road.

When the flat tire hit about a mile down the road, it took everyone by surprise. The car swerved a little, jerking the inhabitants around before Nikki maneuvered to the shoulder.

"I refuse to believe that was a flat, Dominique," her mother said softly. "We're already running a bit late."

"Well, Mom," Nikki replied, unable to stop her chuckle, "I think you're going to have to face facts. Are you all right, Petra?" Nikki shifted to look into the back.

"I didn't like that." Her voice shook a little.

"It was a little scary, wasn't it?"

Petra nodded but didn't cry, and even managed a smile when Nikki reached back to stroke her leg.

"I think I'll get out and have a look," Nikki suggested.

"Watch your dress," Virginia warned.

"I will."

Looking did no good, but getting out in the air helped Nikki to think over her options. They were still quite a distance from any houses or businesses. It was hard to know what to do: head back to the house or try to walk toward town. Petra suddenly spoke before Nikki even realized she'd gotten out of the car.

"We can go back and get my dad's car. He won't mind, Nikki."

"We could, Petra, but even if I walked all the way back, I don't have a key to it."

"He leaves the keys in it."

"Every time?"

"I think so."

Nikki thought it might very well be true, but she wasn't taking a chance.

"How does it look?" Virginia called from the window.

"It looks flat, but I think I should just try to change it."

Her mother was out of the car almost before Nikki could finish speaking.

"Your dress will never survive, Nikki. Maybe if we just wait a little longer . . ."

"What time is it?"

Virginia consulted her watch, and the face she pulled told Nikki they were running very late. Suddenly Nikki wanted to laugh. She bit her lip, but her mirth would not be squelched. Her mother tried to look stern, but it was no use. They giggled for a few moments; it was all so crazy. But light as the mood was, it didn't change the inevitable—a minute later Nikki popped the trunk in order to get at the jack and spare.

❧ ❧ ❧

Dorian told himself that anything could have happened—the car may not have started, Petra could have become ill, anything. It probably wasn't anything very exciting either, but the need to know where his bride was pressed in more strongly by the second. At the moment he was very pleased that they'd opted for a private ceremony—the only people present were Pastor, Tim Warburton, and Theo. No one teased him, but everyone was very aware that the bride was late. Tim hung by the door in order to catch sight of her, and indeed, Dorian had stood with him for a time, but he now walked to the front pew, sat down, and stared at the cross that hung over the baptismal tank.

He was still praying, giving this day to the Lord and asking for His peace, when Theo joined him.

"You're trying not to worry, aren't you, Dad?"

"I am working on that, Theo. It would be very easy to panic right now."

"Should you call the house?"

"I could, but something tells me that if Nikki could get to a phone, she would have called here first."

Dorian looked down at his young face, marveling at how often he acted and spoke beyond his years.

"I think it will be fine, Dad. Nikki's not the type to not come."

"You're right; she's not." There was so much more to that statement than most people would have guessed. It caused Dorian to ask, "Did you think of your mother today?"

Theo nodded.

"Were you sad?"

"No. Nikki is special, and Petra doesn't even remember Mom." Theo looked at his father. "Did you think of Mom?"

"This morning, I did. I thought about the joy and peace the Lord has given me with Nikki, and so I prayed that wherever your mom is, she would turn to the Lord and live for Him."

Theo nodded. "Nikki won't leave us, Dad. I just know she won't."

Dorian smiled. "When did you grow up on me, Theo?"

Theo only smiled, and Dorian put an arm around him. He continued to pray, but not just for himself: There was a little boy waiting with him, whose heart was as involved as his own.

❧ ❧ ❧

"How's it going?"

"Not well," Nikki grunted, a trickle of sweat running down the side of her face. "They make this look so easy on TV, but two of these lug nuts do not want to budge." Nikki came to her feet. She'd been hunkered down so long that her back and legs were cramping. If she could have just dropped to her knees it would have been more comfortable, but her dress was going to be in bad enough shape as it was.

She was taking a deep breath to go at it again when her mother said, "Oh, Nikki, look."

She followed her mother's gaze; a police car was stopping. The sweltering bride could have wept with relief.

"This looks like fun," the tall trooper said with a smile.

"Well, if I could get to the church, I think it might be more fun."

The man stopped. "Dominique Brinks?"

"Yes, how did you know?"

"My daughter reads your books, and you'd have thought it was her own wedding, the way she reacted when she learned the news."

"Can you give us a lift?" Virginia asked. "We're running very late."

"Absolutely. I'll even call road service for you and have this fixed. Where do you want the car delivered?"

"To the Bible Church."

"All right. Hop in, and we'll be there in a few minutes."

Petra had been watching from the backseat and now came leaping out to ride in the state trooper's car. This was almost as much fun as her father marrying Nikki.

There was little Nikki could do with her hands and dress before they arrived, but the moment they pulled up in front of the church, she shot in the door and to the ladies' room to make repairs. When she emerged, Dorian was waiting. He was alone and came right to her. Nikki looked up at him and told herself not to bawl.

"My dress got dirty, and I broke a nail," she whispered.

"I don't care." He had eyes only for her face. "I only care that you're standing in this church and that you're going to become my wife."

Nikki's chest lifted with a huge sigh. "I knew you would be a good sport, Dr. Swann."

Dorian offered his arm. "Come and be my wife, Nikki."

Nikki was a girl who knew a good thing when she saw it; there was no need to ask twice. There was also no need to ask twice when, two hours later, Pastor Andersen asked Nikki to stand up and share her escapade for all at the reception. The natural storyteller emerged, and she had the occupants of the community hall in near hysterics as she told about the flat tire and the policeman's recognition of her.

"His daughter is a big fan. I'd have offered to sign a book for her on the spot if I'd had one along."

With that closing remark she sat back down next to Dorian, who leaned to kiss her. They shared a long look, each telling the other they couldn't wait to be alone.

❧ ❧ ❧

Three weeks later, the honeymoon over and Nikki completely moved in to the big white house, the children were in bed and Nikki was waiting for Dorian to come home. She had known there would be times when she would feel the strong effects of being a doctor's wife, and as she sat on the porch watching for his car, she knew there would be a lifetime of this. There was no anxiety in her, however. Dorian was the kindest man she'd ever known, and even when his patients needed him at inopportune times, knowing that he was coming home to her was comfort enough.

Her heart leaped in her chest when she saw his lights, and she swiftly scooted inside to meet him at the kitchen door. They shared a kiss before Nikki told him she would put his dinner together, but Dorian told her he wasn't hungry.

"I find I just want to hold my wife," he said softly as he led the way to the big chair in the living room. He dropped into it, and Nikki climbed into his lap.

"How was your day?" Nikki was the first to ask this time.

"Busy, but it went well. I've gained some kind of celebrity status now that I'm married to Dominique Brinks."

"Is that right?" Nikki knew when she was being teased.

"Yes, it is. I saw two fourth graders today who had more questions about you than I had time for."

Knowing he would just keep it up, Nikki tried not to smile. Still, a grin peeked through.

"Yes, indeed," the physician went on, having the time of his life. "Me, a small town doctor married to *the* Dominique Brinks. And she even sits in my lap," he added with a mischievous lift of his brows.

Nikki's smile was huge as she tenderly framed Dorian's face in her hands.

"*You* may call me Mrs. Dorian Swann."

And Dorian did, just before he kissed her again.

A Note from Lori: *I love Christmas movies, and just like Nikki, I make myself save them for the holiday season. Irving Berlin's* White Christmas *rates very near the top for me, and it was from the movie that I used the name Pine Tree, Vermont. A careful search of the atlas told me there is no such town, but the name was so wonderful I couldn't resist using it.*

An Intense Man

*But one who looks intently at the perfect law,
the law of liberty, and abides by it, not having
become a forgetful hearer but an effectual doer,
this man shall be blessed in what he does.*

James 1:25

Kelly Donovan pushed the glass office door open and then rubbed her sweating palms together as she tried to calm the frantic beating of her heart. She was convinced at the moment that being a temporary secretary was the worst job in the world—you never knew what you were going to find. She had worked for men and women who were absolute lambs and for others who had given her nightmares long after she'd moved on.

Today and for the next eight weeks she would be working for a Mr. Nicholas Hamilton. He was a successful, high-powered criminal lawyer from a large private firm situated in downtown San Francisco, and he had actually contacted the Amos Secretarial Agency for a fill-in secretary himself. This was very unusual, and Mrs. Kroft, the manager of the agency, had looked at Kelly with a steely glint.

"I don't have to tell you how out-of-the-ordinary this is, Miss Donovan. You are my best secretary, and I cannot stress to you strongly enough that you must not let us down."

Kelly's "Yes, Mrs. Kroft" had been meek but not feigned. She was a very sweet, even-tempered young woman, ready to please, and not given to allowing her life to be ruled by her emotions. This morning, however, she was nervous. Her last job had been almost a month long, but it had felt like a year. The man for whom she had worked had been impossible to please, and as hard as Kelly now worked at remaining calm, her palms still grew damp.

"Who are you?"

A deep voice startled Kelly, and she jumped slightly. She hadn't even seen the other person.

"I'm Kelly Donovan. The Amos Agency sent me."

She was stared at by the owner of the voice as they stood together in the office/waiting room. He was at least 6'3", with very dark hair and startling blue eyes. His chin was determined, stubborn even, and his black brows met in a single line over a long, fine nose. There was a sprinkling of gray at his temples.

"What do you want?" he continued in that same deep tone.

Kelly's hand literally dripped. "I was told you needed someone to do secretarial work; I must have the wrong office."

The man turned away from her then and stared at the empty desk as though just noticing it. Kelly was on the verge of leaving when he spoke, almost to himself.

"She's having a baby."

"I beg your pardon?" Kelly responded, desperately trying to keep up.

"I need a letter," he told her. "Is that what you're here for?"

"Yes, sir."

With that he turned and went into his inner office. Kelly nearly tore her jacket off before frantically scrambling in the desk for a steno pad. In her two years of experience, she found that dictating letters was swiftly dying out, but if Mr. Hamilton wanted to dictate a letter, it was her job to oblige him. It felt like many minutes had passed before she found a pad and pen, but her new employer made no comment and began almost before she could take a seat. The phone rang once during his oration, but since he showed no signs of slowing, Kelly was forced to keep on.

His terse "That will be all" ended the session as abruptly as it had begun, and Kelly retired to the outer desk to try to find her way around the strange computer and file system. She heard nothing from the inner office for the better part of two hours, and when her boss did appear, he looked surprised to see her.

"Did you need something, Mr. Hamilton?"

The tall man stared at her for a moment. "What was your name again?"

"Kelly—Kelly Donovan."

"Yes, right. Well, I need these notes typed before noon."

"Yes, sir."

He left the papers without further word, and Kelly went to work. The phone rang a few times, but no one wanted to speak directly to Mr. Hamilton, so Kelly took messages. At 11:45 she knocked on the heavy oak door and was given permission to enter. She laid the letter from that morning and all the papers on his desk, but he never raised his head.

Kelly had just let herself back into the waiting area when a woman came in. She was puffing like a steam engine and looked as though she was ready to deliver any moment; indeed, it looked like she might be carrying triplets.

"Oh, thank heaven you're still here!" she gasped. "I was told only an hour ago that the woman who was to be here to start you couldn't make it. I'm so glad you stayed."

Kelly only stared, and the woman apologized.

"I'm sorry. I'm Brandy Clemens, Mr. Hamilton's secretary."

"Oh," Kelly replied sympathetically. "I'm sorry you had to come in. I think I'm doing pretty well."

"I know you are," Brandy exclaimed, "or you would have run by now."

"I don't know what you mean," Kelly admitted, and Brandy came to a complete halt.

"I can see that," she began slowly, "which can only mean he's having a good day."

Kelly didn't know how to answer this, but Brandy only smiled at her.

"Okay," she began, and in the next 30 minutes she gave Kelly a rundown on the operations. Kelly tried to absorb everything and then had a few questions. Her heart silently praised God that she had done things right so far, but as Brandy left, she gave Kelly a word of caution.

"Just remember that nothing is personal, Kelly."

"Okay," Kelly said, but her voice told the other woman that she didn't really understand.

Brandy tried again. "He's a very intense man to work for, and if he blows up at you, it's nothing personal. He just has a job to get done and can't see anything else."

Kelly nodded. This was something she could understand, since many of her employers had been the same way. Kelly thanked Brandy, who seemed relieved to be leaving, and returned to her work, but it was several days before Brandy's words were made more than clear to Kelly. Calmly brushing her windblown hair from her face, she walked into the office and was stopped short by her employer's voice.

"Where have you been?" He was coldly furious.

Kelly took a swift glance at her watch; she was ten minutes early.

"Where is the Morgan file?" he bit out. "What have you done with it?"

To Kelly's knowledge she had never seen the file, but she moved swiftly forward.

"I'll check for you."

The desk and files were a mess, and Kelly saw that he'd been rifling through them. She looked swiftly, but having Mr. Hamilton standing there glaring at her made it rather strained, and he was right: The file was nowhere to be found.

"Could it be on your desk, Mr. Hamilton?" Kelly finally ventured.

The look she received was frightening, and his voice was angrier than ever.

"Fine! If it will satisfy your curiosity, go ahead and look." His hand swept toward the door, but it was not a nice gesture.

Kelly had no idea how to respond to his sarcasm, but she entered his office on shaking legs. In some ways she hoped the file wouldn't be there, as it was sure to put him in a worse humor. She looked anyway and produced the file in less than a minute.

"Is this the one, Mr. Hamilton?"

"Yes, Miss Donally." His voice was still terse. "I'll be in court for the remainder of the week."

If Kelly had been able to see herself in the mirror at that moment, she would have seen a shaken redhead whose green eyes and freckles stood out starkly on her pale face. Her heart felt slightly crushed and beaten. It took a few minutes to remember Brandy's advice. With the thought, Kelly's chin rose ever so slightly.

"My name's not Donally," she spoke softly to the empty room. "It's Donovan. Kelly Donovan."

❧ ❧ ❧

The next eight weeks were a roller coaster ride. Some days flew by and others dragged. Some days Mr. Hamilton was absentminded and kind, and others he was intense, rude, and overbearing.

Kelly's good friend, Jill, was a constant help during those weeks. She was never too busy to listen, and she and her new husband, Russell, had Kelly over to dinner several times.

"He was a terror today," Kelly told them one night, her voice a bit sad. "He finally knows my name, but I couldn't do anything right."

"I've been praying that you'll have an opportunity to witness to him, Kelly," Russell told her. "But I think maybe I should pray that you'll just survive."

Kelly chuckled. "It does feel that way at times. The money has been good—I've put quite a bit away for lean times—but I'm so glad that I'll be done next week." Kelly looked at Jill, her face guilty. "I sound terribly ungrateful, don't I?"

Jill squeezed her hand. "I think the Lord understands. It hasn't been easy for you."

"Does the agency have something lined up for you next week?" Russell asked.

"Yes," Kelly told them with a pleased smile. "That candy company on Parker Street needs a temp. I'm scheduled there for three weeks."

"That will be a nice break for you," Russell said.

"I hope so," Kelly returned, her smile still in place. "I hope the biggest problem will be staying out of the chocolate."

"It's a tough job," Russell winked at her, "but someone's got to do it."

&. &. &.

"Now, on Monday," Mr. Hamilton began firmly but not unkindly, "I'll be in court with the—"

"Brandy will be back on Monday," Kelly gently cut in.

The intense lawyer looked at her as though he'd just noticed she was there and then said, "I need you in court, Kelly."

The redhead nodded. "Brandy is going to call me this weekend so I can explain everything to her."

Again the stare.

"You'll win this case," Kelly told him simply and was pleased to see him look surprised. "Especially if Brandy is back. I'll type these notes for you now." With that she exited and felt very thankful that her last day was going to be pleasant. And indeed, it almost was, but with only an hour of work left, a call came in from his key witness that set her employer on a rampage.

Barked at and berated for the remainder of the day, Kelly left for home feeling like a limp rag. She didn't cry—she was too tired to make the effort—but with a weary heart she thanked God she would never have to see Nicholas Hamilton again.

❧ ❧ ❧

Eight Months Later

"Okay," Kelly instructed the small charges from her Sunday school class, "we're going out on the lawn today to look for things God has made. I don't want you to sit on the grass in your good clothes or walk in the flower beds. Does everyone understand?"

Eight four-year-olds nodded their heads as their small eyes watched her with love. Kelly smiled at them and pushed the door open. A man was coming in, one who held the door wide, but Kelly thanked him without looking up. She wouldn't have raised her head at all if she hadn't heard, "You're welcome, Kelly."

Her green eyes shot up and found Mr. Hamilton watching her. He looked much the same as he had eight months ago—tall, handsome, and impeccably dressed—but today there was a difference.

"Hello," Kelly murmured faintly, receiving a small smile in return.

"Miss Donovan, Crissy's in the flowers."

Kelly had no choice but to move away and take care of her students, but it took a few moments for her to remember why they'd come outside at all. The remainder of the class time passed in a type of haze, and Kelly's former boss was still heavy on her mind when the church service started. When the singing was over and the sermon actually began, Kelly forced her mind to the words at hand. In fact, she had so successfully put Mr. Hamilton from her mind that her mouth actually swung open when at two o'clock that afternoon she answered the knock at her front door and found him standing there.

"Mr. Hamilton," she said inanely.

"Hello, Kelly. I knocked on two wrong doors before I found you."

"Oh," she said rather stupidly and then recalled her manners. "Would you like to come in?"

He entered without comment, and Kelly invited him to sit down. He chose her most uncomfortable chair but didn't seem to notice. Kelly sat across from him, her heart pounding with anticipation.

"I didn't know you went to that church," Nicholas began.

Kelly smiled. "I didn't know you did either."

"This is only my second week. I came to Christ ten days ago."

Kelly bit her lip and pressed the fingernails of one hand into her palm to keep from crying. His face was serene yet excited. Kelly felt a tremendous rush of emotions.

"Tell me how it happened," she finally said and thought it was much like uncorking a bottle.

"I was miserable," he admitted. "I couldn't understand why I was restless and angry. I had everything I needed, but I was still impossible to please. My brother told me I needed help. I thought he was talking about a shrink, but then he took me to see Roger Foy."

"Pastor Foy?" Kelly asked. "Pastor North's assistant?"

"Yes. I expected him to tell me how much money I needed to give to the church in order to find happiness, but he didn't say that. He said you have to be born again. I laughed in his face. I told him I'd already been born once, but then he opened his Bible and showed me where Jesus had said that to Nicodemus.

"I was flabbergasted by the story he read me as well as the words. I'd never understood the Bible before, but this was in plain English and not at all cryptic. I mean, Jesus himself said that we can't see heaven unless we first accept God's gift of life. I didn't know that. It's funny, but I've always believed that Jesus was God—I just didn't know He'd said all these things.

"And I have to tell you the craziest part: I really didn't think it would work. My prayer was sincere, but I didn't think it could really be that easy. I kept waiting for Roger to tell me I could write out my check now. Instead, he offered to meet with me every week for discipleship, and he even gave me his home phone number and said I could call at any time of the day or night."

Kelly smiled. "He's like that—always available."

"Have you known, Kelly?" Nick's face was very serious. "Have you known about Christ for a long time?"

"Since I was 13."

"So you've read the Bible a lot."

Kelly nodded.

"Can you tell me what Pastor North was talking about when he mentioned the Davidic Covenant?"

And with that they were off. Kelly brought out her Bible, and they talked and discussed the Scriptures for hours. Mr. Hamilton was a brilliant man, and there were times when Kelly felt like she was out of her league, but anything she couldn't tell him he simply wrote down in a small notebook to ask Roger later. Kelly was utterly amazed to look at her watch and find that it was after five o'clock.

"Oh, look at the time!" she exclaimed. "Would you like something to eat, Mr. Hamilton?"

"No, thank you, I'm not hungry. I read a verse yesterday . . ." and he was off again.

Kelly didn't know how to handle this. The evening service started in 45 minutes, and she really would have liked a sandwich but told herself she could wait. However, she did not want to miss the service. When her watch read 5:30, Kelly plunged in.

"Are you going to the evening service, Mr. Hamilton?"

He stared at her, thoroughly nonplused. "You go to church at night?"

Kelly nodded. "Six o'clock. My ride will be here in a few minutes."

"Oh, well, I can take you, and then we can talk on the way."

Again Kelly wasn't sure how to field this ball, but she decided swiftly, and the next few minutes were spent in a flurry as she made a phone call, changed her clothes, and rushed out the door to Nick's long sports car. They sat together during the service, and afterward he had more questions about what he'd heard. Pastor Foy saw them talking and came to join them. The church slowly closed down while the three stood in the parking lot and talked.

It was after 8:30 when Nick said, "Well, you've given me a lot to think about. I'm going to go home now and look up these verses in James. Goodnight, Roger. Night, Kelly." And with that he was gone. Kelly watched him, praying he would remember her, but a moment later his Jaguar roared to life and he was gone.

"He's very excited, isn't he?"

"Yes," Kelly agreed. "It's a joy to watch him. He's as intense with this as he is with everything else."

"Yes. Well, I'd better scoot. Jana has gone onto the Brennan's and will think I'm lost. Goodnight, Kelly."

"Goodnight, Pastor."

Kelly stood motionless for a moment, her mind going over the easiest walk home. With the hills in San Francisco, it was going to be a climb. She was thankful that she was in slacks and low-heeled shoes. Suddenly Pastor Foy's car pulled up alongside of her.

"I forgot that you don't have a car, Kelly; how did you get here tonight?"

Kelly smiled. "With Mr. Hamilton."

"Oh, no," Roger said on a laugh as he shook his head. "Hop in. We'll swing by the Brennans', get Jana, and run you home."

Kelly climbed in with a word of thanks.

"Do you think Nick will be calling on you again?" Roger asked as the car pulled into the street.

"I don't know," Kelly replied with a smile in her voice, "but if he does, you'd better pray for me. He asked me questions today that I've never even thought of."

Roger laughed. "You'll do fine, but if you do end up over your head, just pick up the phone, Kelly."

Again she thanked him, and even though she hated to inconvenience him and his wife, she appreciated the offer and the ride home.

※ ※ ※

"I tried to call you today at that car place, but they said you were gone."

No hello or greeting of any kind. Kelly smiled to herself as she held her apartment door wide and waited for Nick to enter. She had told him she was not going to be at Talmont Buick after last week, but he had not heard her.

"I want to know what you think of this animal in Job, this behemoth. Let's go get some dinner and talk about it."

Kelly hesitated as she always did when he mentioned eating out.

"Why don't I fix us something here?" she finally asked.

Nick shook his head. "I'm in the mood for a steak."

She sighed very gently. "I'll get my coat."

Kelly didn't know how it had begun, but the first time they'd eaten a meal together, not wanting to presume, she'd pulled forth her wallet when the check arrived. Nick had never even blinked when she offered to pay for her share, and it had been like that ever since. So now, whenever he asked her for a meal, she had to do quick sums in her head to see if she could afford it. She couldn't right now, but it wasn't the first time she had settled for a salad or cup of soup while Nick enjoyed a full-course meal. He never noticed her meager portions in his effort to gain more answers about Scripture or tell her what he'd learned that week. Kelly thought she could have talked to him about her finances at the beginning, but this had been the pattern for nine months now, and she simply didn't know how.

"I think the animal in Job 40:15 is a dinosaur," Kelly told him as she tried to make her soup into a meal.

"Why?"

"Well, for one thing, it says he's got a tail like a cedar. All other Scripture references to cedars are the cedars of Lebanon, and they're huge. The tail on this animal is like a full-grown redwood. That could only be a dinosaur."

He fell into a thoughtful silence that continued even when the waiter appeared with a carafe of coffee. Kelly had to speak to him twice.

"Mr. Hamilton, would you like coffee?"

"Oh! Yes, please," he replied in a startled voice. After Kelly had creamed hers, she looked up to find him staring at her—really looking—for the first time.

"Do you always call me Mr. Hamilton?"

Kelly nodded.

"Why?"

"Well, that's what I called you when I worked for you, and I still just do." Kelly shrugged helplessly.

"Well, you don't work for me anymore. Why don't you call me Nick?"

"All right," Kelly said softly and worked at hiding her pleasure.

"Is that a new blouse?" he asked.

"No." Again Kelly's voice was soft; she had owned the blouse for two years.

"It's a nice color."

"Thank you."

It was the first time he had been even remotely personal with her, and Kelly took a sip of her coffee in order to hide her emotions.

At this rate, she said to herself, not knowing if she wanted to laugh or cry, *he'll ask me to marry him in just under ten years.*

🦋 🦋 🦋

"Are you going to the wedding, Nick?"

"What wedding?"

"Gina North is getting married. It was in the bulletin."

"Oh, yes, I saw that. I think so."

"Could I get a ride?"

"Certainly."

It was risky business going with him because she never knew when he was going to forget her, but she wanted very much to attend with him.

They were in another restaurant, and this time Kelly had enough cash for soup *and* a salad. It was one year to the day that Nick had knocked on her door, but only Kelly was aware of this anniversary of sorts. Everyone at church thought they were an item: everyone but Nick, Kelly, and Jill. Jill had been the one to see Kelly's tears.

"I must not be the type men fall in love with, Jill. I mean, Russell fell for you the moment he set eyes on you. In a year's time, I've been given permission to call him by his first name, and I've seen his house twice." The tears had spilled over then, and Jill had hugged her. "I tell myself to move on, but I don't think he would even notice."

"Have you noticed," Nick's voice brought her back to the moment, "how many times Paul prays for grace for the believers of the early church? I haven't been doing that, I mean, praying for grace, but I think it is significant."

"I think you're right," Kelly agreed with him. "Grace is everything for salvation, but we couldn't live for Christ without grace. His grace frees us to serve Him and return for fellowship and renewal time and again."

They talked on for the next hour, and when Nick dropped Kelly off, she reminded him of the wedding.

"What wedding?"

Kelly stared at him. "I'll get a ride with Jill and Russell."

"All right," he agreed so swiftly that Kelly felt crushed. A moment later he said goodnight and was gone. Kelly told herself not to cry, but she couldn't help it.

"Should I move away, Lord?" she sobbed. "Should I tell him how I feel? I feel my heart can't take anymore."

It was a steamy night, so Kelly stepped into a cool shower and let the tears flow. She didn't really have any answers, but she felt better, and when she finally climbed into bed, slept almost immediately.

❧ ❧ ❧

Russell and Jill had just arrived to get Kelly on Saturday when Nick's Lincoln pulled up to a silent halt before the apartment. Russell and Jill were not surprised to see him, so they only smiled at the look Kelly gave them and pulled away.

"I thought you were riding with me," Nick said as she neared, having watched the other couple drive away.

"I wasn't certain," Kelly answered after deciding not to explain. Nick didn't comment further, and after Kelly climbed in, they were on their way.

The wedding was lovely. So that Pastor North could walk his daughter down the aisle as well as perform the ceremony, both pastors were involved. The whole congregation cheered when the newlyweds turned and were presented to the assembly as husband and wife. The reception was right at the church, and everyone was in high spirits as they followed the wedding party over for a lovely meal. Kelly couldn't remember when she'd had so much fun, but a dark cloud was looming.

They had been through the reception line and had just eaten, when Mrs. Casmont, one of the older ladies, approached. She zeroed in on Nick, and a moment later the fun went out of their afternoon.

"Has this given you some ideas, Nick?"

"I don't know what you mean," he replied sincerely.

"Why, marriage of course. It's time you settle down. You and Kelly aren't getting any younger."

Nick, who had greatly matured in the Lord over the previous year, tried to smile, but Kelly could see that it was strained. She wanted to tell Mrs. Casmont to move on her way, but there was no way to do this gently. That her treatment of them was not gentle in the first place made no difference. Kelly felt humiliated, but she was not going to lash out in return.

"Well, I only hope this has given you some ideas," she said again, trying to be coy. "It would be so exciting if you could make that announcement today, but well ..." She gave a dramatic sigh, and Kelly gave one herself when she finally moved away.

"Let's go, Kelly." Nick's terse voice came to her ears just a moment later, and Kelly swiftly made her goodbyes.

In the car Nick said nothing. Kelly felt tense with the strain and even more so when he didn't take her home. It took a moment for her to see that he was headed to his own house. He still hadn't spoken when he parked in the spacious garage, climbed from behind the wheel, and started toward the door. Kelly felt she had no choice but to follow. They were in Nick's elegant living room when he exploded.

"I'm not the marrying kind! Mrs. Casmont had no business speaking to us in that way. It's none of her affair!"

Kelly said nothing since he wasn't really talking to her.

"And you just stood there!"

Suddenly under attack, Kelly was stunned.

"What was I supposed to do?" she asked, but he was raking his hand through his hair and didn't hear her.

"Of all the interfering, rude women I've ever known, she just about takes the cake. And *you* probably put her up to it."

If Nick had been looking at Kelly, he'd have seen her stunned look of disbelief and pain. Tears that she simply couldn't keep at bay flooded her eyes. Nick chose that moment to look.

Kelly blinked furiously in an effort to control herself and just barely managed. Nick was silent but pacing.

After a moment Kelly said, "Maybe I should go."

"Yes," Nick still didn't look at her. "I need to think."

Still too shaken to speak, Kelly let herself quietly out the door. Unlike being stranded at the church, she was miles from home, but she began walking anyway. She wanted to cry her eyes out, but she had to keep her head until she arrived home. Kelly had walked nearly a mile when Nick's car pulled up. The passenger-side window went down.

"Come on, Kelly, I'll give you a ride home."

His voice sounded normal, but Kelly shook her head.

"No. I'll walk."

"Come on, Kelly," he ordered, but again she refused.

"I don't want to be yelled at anymore." With that she walked on and barely noticed when Nick's car pulled smoothly ahead of her and parked at the curb. By the time she reached him, he'd climbed from his seat and was holding the door open on her side.

"I won't yell at you anymore. Please get in."

Kelly looked at him and realized she was trembling.

"Please, Kelly." His voice was soft.

Finally, she went to the car. Kelly was so tense that she barely let her back rest against the seat as he pulled from the curb and drove her home. She was thankful that he didn't speak to her, but when he stopped in front of her apartment, she spoke with quiet conviction without ever looking at him.

"If you think I actually put Mrs. Casmont up to that, then you don't know me at all."

"I don't think that," he admitted just as quietly. "I was upset."

Kelly nodded and opened the door. Nick spoke while she was still climbing out.

"Do you want me to come in?"

Again Kelly couldn't look at him. "No," her voice broke on a sob, "I don't."

She closed the car door, and Nick watched as she rushed for her apartment. He stared out the windshield for a moment, knowing he had to make things right. He glanced around and found a parking place. A few minutes later he was standing before Kelly's door. He raised his hand to knock but saw that it was slightly open. With a gentle push, he entered. He heard the evidence of Kelly's tears long before he saw them, and something painful and tight squeezed around his chest. His footsteps sounded on the floor, and she jumped in surprise. She swiftly rose from where she'd been sitting at the kitchen table and wiped at her face.

"Kelly," Nick began, but she shook her head, and he stopped. Kelly forced herself to turn and face him. She looked at him for the space of several moments and then began to speak.

"It's all for you. This whole relationship is all for you." She sniffed, but her voice spoke of her resolve without being harsh. "The whole church thinks we're an item. What a joke! You have this big family that you share the holidays with. I spent Christmas, Thanksgiving, and Easter alone, Nick, because everyone assumed you'd asked me to join you." She could see that she'd shocked and upset him but kept on anyway.

"I never call you. I never bother you. I wait for you to be in touch, and when you are, you never ask how Kelly is doing. It's all for Nick. If I have trouble making ends meet, I don't say a word for fear that you'll think I'm asking for money. I do everything in my power to make you feel cared for and encouraged, and now I'm accused of trying to trap you into marriage."

Kelly gasped a little now because the tears were coming back. She turned slightly away so Nick wouldn't see them. After a moment she spoke, this time very quietly.

"I think I'd like you to go, Nick. I need some time alone."

She watched from the corner of her eyes as he hesitated, but a moment later he turned for the door. Kelly went to that portal when she heard it close and this time made sure it was locked. She got no farther than the sofa in the living room before the tears came in a flood once again.

❧ ❧ ❧

"Well, Nick! Come on in. We've just arrived home from the wedding."

"Can I talk to you, Roger?"

"Certainly. Let's go into the family room."

They made themselves comfortable, but Nick didn't talk. Roger was not a man given to light conversation, so he waited patiently. It took several moments before Nick began. He relayed the entire day's events, his voice troubled and confused.

"And then she asked me to leave. I wanted to stay. I wanted to tell her I was sorry, but she was crying. I've never seen her cry. Is she right, Roger? Am I that self-centered? Is the whole relationship for me?"

Roger looked at him for a moment. "Tell me, Nick, how often do you see Kelly?"

Nick shrugged. "I don't know."

"Every week?" Roger prompted. "Every month? More then once a week? How often?"

"I guess every week."

Roger smiled a little. "You and I meet every week, and have for more than a year, but you never mention her. Jana has told me that she sees the two of you together, but I don't see you together that often, and since you never talk about her, I've never given it any thought. You've grown so much Nick, but being a new Christian is almost like being an infant. Your world starts out very small, and the only person you can take care of is yourself. It sounds like that's how it's been for you.

"And Kelly, well, I don't know her very well, but I know she wouldn't do anything that might discourage you or make you stumble. It sounds like whatever has been going on in the past is too much for her right now. Because I'm not involved, you would be the best judge of whether or not you're treating Kelly with love."

Nick's eyes slid shut. How did you treat someone with love when the only person you saw was yourself? Nick's heart clenched in pain. He looked at his watch. It was only half past four. He still had time. He stood, and Roger asked where he was going.

"To make things right" was all Nick said, and after thanking Roger, he was swiftly on his way.

🌰 🌰 🌰

Kelly was dozing in a chair when Nick knocked on her door. It never occurred to her that he would return, so she was totally unsuspecting, but there he was, still dressed in his suit and holding an enormous bouquet of flowers. Kelly's heart hurt just to look at him, and her voice was soft.

"You didn't have to do this, Nick."

"Yes, I did," he told her, and then saw that his words had upset her. "I wanted to," he rushed to say. "I wanted to buy these for you."

Kelly looked up at him and then reached for the flowers.

"Thank you," she said.

"May I come in, Kelly?"

Kelly looked away. "I don't know if that's a good idea, Nick." She still felt bruised.

"I have something to say," he told her. "If you want me to leave after that, I will, but will you please hear me out?"

After a moment Kelly stepped aside. Nick entered and went to her living room but didn't sit down. He paced nervously in the small space and then turned to her.

"I went to see Roger Foy," he admitted. "I asked him if what you said was true, and it is, Kelly, it is. I never think of anyone but myself."

Kelly had to bite her lip, or she was going to cry again. He looked so shaken and distressed. She had felt awful after he left, fearing that she had said something to make him doubt God's love, and now to have him looking so vulnerable was almost too much for her. His next words threatened to break her heart.

"You're my best friend, Kelly. Even as a kid I thought the concept of best friends was ridiculous, but I realized that's just what you are. You care for me and listen to me, and I've just used you. I don't know if you can ever forgive me, Kelly, but I'm sorry."

"Oh, Nick, of course I forgive you, and I'm sorry I talked to you that way."

"Don't apologize, Kelly," he said sternly. "You need to hold me accountable. If I'm not treating you well, you'd best tell me in a hurry."

Kelly nodded and smiled at him. They talked for a few more minutes before he asked if she wanted to go for a bite to eat, but Nick was gracious when Kelly told him that it had been an emotional day and that she was going to turn in early. She had already cried so much that she had a headache, but the tears came again when Nick was gone

He says I'm his best friend, she told the Lord. *I want to hear "I love you, Kelly" but find that I'm his best friend. I must move on, Lord. I'm waiting for Nick to love me, and that's not going to happen. Please show me a way to survive this and grow. Please help me to still be there for Nick without losing my mind.*

Kelly prayed in such a manner for more than an hour, and as sometimes happens, an affirmative answer came immediately. The phone rang as she was readying for bed. It was a young man who had been out of the area for a few years. He'd gotten her phone number from someone at church and wanted to know if she was free for dinner on Friday night. Kelly accepted before she could talk herself out of it, and even though her heart beat with anxiety, she was asleep five minutes after she'd climbed into bed.

❧ ❧ ❧

Kelly leaned close to the mirror and examined the corners of her eyes for wrinkles. She was going to be 24 in a month and was convinced that she looked closer to 40. She was mumbling about what Peter would think of her when she heard the knock.

"Oh! Nick!" Kelly said as she opened the front door and then recovered swiftly. "How are you?"

"I'm all right," he said as he came in, "but I need to talk to you about—" He stopped when he saw the way she was dressed. "Is this a bad time?"

"Well, actually I'm going to be leaving."

"Oh." Nick looked at ease. "I'll go with you."

"Well," Kelly tried again, thinking she would cut her own hand off before she deliberately hurt him. "I'm going to dinner."

"With Jill? She never minds when I come along."

Kelly was still trying to frame a reply when a second knock sounded. She opened the door, and Peter was standing there. He was smiling, but his eyes looked uncertain when he saw Nick.

"Do I have the wrong night, Kelly?"

"No, Peter. Nick just needed to ask me something. You've met, haven't you?"

"Of course," Nick offered, stepping into the breach. He moved forward, shook Peter's hand, and greeted him warmly. "We met at church on Sunday and then at men's prayer breakfast this week. How are you?"

"Fine. Did I interrupt something?"

"No, no," Nick assured him magnanimously, but Kelly thought he sounded odd. "I'll catch Kelly on Sunday. You two have a good time."

Goodbyes were said, and everyone went in opposite directions. Back in his car, Nick pulled away from the apartment building but drove only down the street to the parking lot of the grocery store, where he put the car in park and sat.

"She has a date," he told the windshield. "She's never had a date before. Peter is going to take her out to dinner. She's not doing this to make me jealous since she wasn't even going to tell me about it, so why am I jealous? Why do I feel like a child whose toy has been snatched away?" Nick's brows drew together in self-directed anger, and this time he didn't speak aloud.

She's not a toy, Nick Hamilton, and you're a fool to think of her in such a way. She's a woman with needs, and you haven't been there. If you don't like her seeing someone else, then you'd better make your claim and treat her the way she deserves to be treated.

Nick's pep talk continued for some minutes longer as he prayed and made plans.

Now sitting in a restaurant across from Peter, Kelly was totally unsuspecting that an intense man's thoughts were consumed with her, and that he had plans to change their relationship entirely.

⚘ ⚘ ⚘

"Public library, this is Kelly. May I help you?"

"You most certainly may. You can take pity on me and have dinner with me tonight."

Kelly smiled and laughed a little. It was a week after her date with Peter, and she hadn't heard from Nick since that night. It was lovely to hear his voice.

"All right. What did you have in mind?"

"Let's dress up."

Kelly was sorry she'd asked. Her pocketbook really couldn't take a "dress up" dinner, but she was given no time to reply.

"A call just came in, so I've got to go. I'll pick you up at 6:30." A moment later the connection was broken.

I'll just have to tell him, Kelly told herself firmly, knowing even as she thought it that she probably never would.

❧ ❧ ❧

Kelly knew that Nick had come directly from work when she stepped out of her apartment and saw that the limo was waiting. He had picked her up in this luxurious fashion from time to time, and it always caused a stir in her "old city" neighborhood.

They talked companionably for the next 20 minutes until Kelly realized the driver was taking them to the Parker Club. It was the most exclusive restaurant in San Francisco, and Kelly felt panic coming on. Nick was turning to say something to her, but she grabbed his arm.

"Oh, Nick, I should have said something. I can't afford this. I mean, I really *can't*! I couldn't even get a soup or salad here, Nick. I'm sorry."

"I'm taking care of this," he cut in gently when Kelly paused for a breath, but she only panicked a little more.

"You don't have to pay for my friendship, Nick. I'm sorry if I said anything that made you feel that way. You really don't—" The words were effectively cut off when Nick gently grasped her jaw in one long-fingered hand, forcing Kelly's eyes to look at him.

"I'm not trying to buy your friendship; you know me better than that. Now will you please let me do this?"

"My clothes—"

"Are fine," Nick finished for her. "Now will you please let me buy you dinner?"

It took a moment more. Kelly's eyes searched Nick's in an effort to read his thoughts, and she finally nodded her consent. They climbed from the deep interior of the

limo where Marcos, the driver, stood smiling at them.
Nick spoke a few words to him and then took Kelly's
elbow and moved her to the entrance. They were
treated like royalty. If Kelly's dress and shoes were not
up to par, no one even dared to notice since she was
with Nicholas Hamilton.

The napkin was placed across her lap by a hovering
waiter, and a menu the size of a road atlas was opened
and offered into her hands. Kelly entertained the silly
thought of being grateful that she'd done her nails
when she got home and tried to ignore the fact that
there were no prices. She was doing a lousy job of
trying to act as though she belonged when one of
Nick's fingers curled over the top of her menu, and he
pulled it down so he could see her face.

"Just as I thought," he spoke gently, his eyes amused.
"You're about to panic."

"I feel a little out of my depth, Nick. I'm sorry."

The smile he gave her was very tender. "How
hungry are you?"

"At the moment, I'm not hungry at all."

Again the smile appeared as the menu was taken
from her damp palms, and Nick's finger went in the air.
A waiter appeared as if by magic, and Nick ordered an
appetizer and something to drink. That was it. He
then began a conversation meant to soothe. It must
have worked, because Kelly was halfway through the
plate of tiny crab puffs before she remembered where
she was.

"Where is your family, Kelly?" Nick asked at one
point, having already confessed to the Lord that he'd
never asked before.

"Well, I don't really have any. I was raised in a series of foster homes until I was 12, and then I was placed with a family who kept me."

"Where are they now?"

Kelly smiled. "In Brazil. They decided to go to the mission field when I finished high school. I saw them two years ago, and we write all the time."

"Is it too painful to tell me why you were in foster homes?"

"No, but it's a sad story. I was seven when my mother went to the store and never came home. I went to a neighbor who kept me until dinner, but she called the police when darkness fell. They were able to track some of my mother's movements. Earlier that day she was seen going into a bar and then later getting into a man's car, but that was the end of the trail. They don't think she was forced, and later I realized she had never planned to return."

"That is sad," Nick said, his voice low. "I can't imagine her leaving you alone." Suddenly his face turned very serious. "But *I've* done that often enough, haven't I?"

Kelly didn't answer.

"No more, Kelly," he told her almost fiercely. "I'm not going to treat you like that any longer."

Kelly had dreamed of how it might be to have Nick's intensity directed at her, and now that it had happened, she found it a little frightening. He wanted to know everything about her. And the way he looked at her! Kelly felt like a rocket had shot up her spine.

"Have you always had red hair?"

"Yes. Although it's gotten darker. Occasionally someone would ask me where I got it, and I would say that the postman delivered it."

Nick laughed. "Your father?"

"I never knew him. I had an uncle who came to visit me once, but he didn't stay for more than a few minutes. I was told later that he was really looking for my mother. What is your family like, Nick? I mean, you've talked about them some, but only in reference to salvation."

"Well, my brother Tony is saved, I think you knew that. He doesn't go to our church, but he was the one who introduced me to Roger. Anyway, he's two years younger than I am, and then there's Kevin, and the youngest is my sister, B.J."

"And your folks live in the Bay Area too?"

"Yes, in Burlingame. I grew up there."

"How did you get to San Francisco?"

"I went to law school at Stanford, and when a job opened up here, I jumped at it."

The whole evening continued this way. Nick ordered items off the menu one at a time, and they talked. They learned things about each other they'd never known before, and the hours flew. Kelly started to yawn over dessert, and Nick knew it was time to call it a night. He held her hand on the way home and walked her to her door. Kelly thanked him quietly, and Nick only leaned against the jamb and stared at her face. He didn't know exactly when he'd fallen for this woman, but his heart was gone. Right now he couldn't remember saying he was not the marrying kind. He finally bid Kelly goodnight and wandered back to the limo. It was a good thing Marcos was driving; he'd have never found the way home.

❧ ❧ ❧

"This is the book I'm reading right now," Nick mentioned as he entered his own kitchen where Kelly was in the process of making a green salad. Roger, Jana, Russell, and Jill were all coming to dinner, and Kelly had come early to help. She looked at the title and then at the man holding it.

"You're reading a book about sexual happiness in marriage?"

"Yes. I've read two, and this is my third."

Incredulous, Kelly stared at him, the salad forgotten. "Why?" she finally managed.

"Well, it's important."

"For what?"

"For marriage," he told her simply and frowned at her lack of understanding.

"You're getting married?"

Now he really frowned. "Of course I'm getting married."

Kelly put the lettuce down and started to turn away. Nick caught her hand, but she would not come to him. In fact, she pulled her hand away and moved to the other side of the island to put some space between them.

She looked at him squarely and asked quietly, "Whom are you marrying?"

"*Whom am I marrying?*" he nearly shouted at her. "*I'm marrying you!*" His eyes were huge with shock, but Kelly didn't feel like laughing.

"Were you going to let me in on this?"

"Kelly," he responded in his lawyer's voice, "I talked to you about this; I know I did."

"A woman," she began with a measured tone, "does not forget when a man has talked marriage to her. You haven't said a thing, Nick."

He looked totally bewildered, his mouth opening and closing, but at that moment the doorbell rang. Kelly was completely shaken and stayed in the kitchen. She heard Nick greet both couples and then show them into the living room. When he got back to the kitchen, Kelly was once again working over the salad. Nick came up and put his arms around her. It was the first time he'd done anything more than hold her hand. Kelly turned in his embrace.

"You don't want to marry me," he stated softly.

"I didn't say that, Nick; I just said you didn't ask me."

"And if I asked you now?"

Kelly looked into his eyes. "There's a little fear in me that I'm just what you're *into* right now. I worry that as soon as we're married, and that's taken care of, I'll be yesterday's news."

"Then we need to wait awhile," he told her immediately, "so I can show you that's not going to happen."

"And you're willing to wait?"

"Forever," he told her and leaned to kiss her for the first time.

Kelly's heart sighed. How long had she waited and prayed for this, and now her heart was uncertain.

"Are you going to be all right?" Nick wanted to know.

Kelly nodded and looked into his eyes. What she saw there gave her hope and joy. *I am going to be fine,* she told herself. *In fact, everything is going to be wonderful.*

❧ ❧ ❧

"You're being intense, Nick," Kelly told her husband of almost two years. It was certainly not the first time she had said it during that time, but he always took it in and tried to adjust; indeed, she was very proud of the man he had become.

"How am I being intense this time?"

"I know you have a thirst for knowledge, but I think 15 books on the growth and development of infants is a little extreme."

"Yes, it is," he agreed with her.

Kelly now had to fight laughter. "And then yesterday you told the doctor that I always sleep on my right side and asked if I should switch to my left."

He looked very contrite.

She was smiling when she said, "I worry about you, Nick. The baby isn't due for two weeks, and I'm not sure you're going to make it."

Nick nodded. "Roger talked to me about it too."

"He did?" Kelly was surprised.

"Yes. Lately it's all I've talked about, and he's come to recognize the signs."

Kelly reached up and cupped his cheek. Nick covered his hand with her own, and they leaned simultaneously to kiss. It was during this lovely distraction that Kelly's first pain hit. She jerked and looked so surprised that Nick nearly panicked.

"What is it?"

"I think I'm starting labor."

"It's not supposed to happen yet," Nick exclaimed, voicing Kelly's own thoughts as the pain subsided.

With an effort, Kelly very calmly reminded him that this might not be the real thing.

However, she was wrong. Four hours later Kelly was in so much constant pain that Nick was calling the doctor and rushing her to the hospital. Forty-five minutes after they arrived, Kelly delivered a beautiful baby girl. She was round and pink, and her parents were utterly taken with her. For the first time Kelly had a taste of what intensity felt like.

"Have you ever seen anything so tiny in your whole life?" The new mother asked as she held up the baby's right pinky for inspection. Nick enjoyed the tiny digit as well, but Kelly suddenly covered the small hand with her own.

"I can't stand the thought that she'll go off to school in a few years, Nick. And then after that, the time will just race." She looked at the hand again. "Some man will put a ring on this finger and take her away from us forever."

Kelly nearly had herself in tears, but Nick was just barely holding his laughter.

"How dare you laugh at this, Nicholas Hamilton!"

"Kelly," Nick gasped when he could hold it in no longer. "Which one of us is being intense now?"

Kelly's mouth dropped open with surprise, and then she laughed herself. Her whole body convulsed, causing the baby to start. She finished with a long sigh, her eyes on her husband.

"I never really understood, did I?"

"No, but that's all right. A little intensity is good, especially for each other, and a lot of intensity is great, if it's directed toward Christ." They smiled at each other, and Nick said, "We'll just keep at it, Kelly, until we both get it right."

They leaned across their daughter and kissed. The nurse headed into the room to check on Kelly and the baby, backed out slowly, and closed the door behind her.

"Aren't you going in?" another nurse in the hall asked.

"No. They're having a little time with their baby, and what I need to do can wait."

The other nurse smiled. "It's like that with all first-time parents. Intense for a time, but then it passes."

Kelly's nurse didn't comment as the other woman moved off, but she didn't agree. The experienced nurse had seen something special in that room over the last few hours. She couldn't have put a name to it, but she knew it wasn't going to pass away.

A Note from Lori: *Having grown up in Santa Rosa, California, I've spent many hours in San Francisco. I lived in California until I was 26 years old, so I've experienced the cable cars, dined in the wharf area, seen the aquarium and the Exploratorium, and of course, gone down Lombard Street. In fact, I recently did some of those things with my own children. I'm not familiar with all of "The City" as locals call it, and San Francisco has done a lot of changing, but it was fun to picture Nick and Kelly in the city I remember.*

The Camping Trip

The heavens are telling of the glory of God;
and their expanse is declaring the work of His hands.
Psalm 19:1

❧ ❧ ❧

"Mom, you're not even trying," Chad Farrell said in mild disgust, throwing himself down in the nearest chair.

"What exactly did you want me to do, Chad?" Hilary Farrell asked her 13-year-old son.

"My coach is a Christian."

"So you've said, but you also mentioned the fact that he's nearing 60."

"No," Chad replied with some frustration. "That's the assistant coach. The head coach, Coach Maxwell, is only in his forties."

"Forties or not, honey, don't get your hopes up. I've told you before, Chad, men my age are not looking for a woman whose car won't start most mornings and whose house still has a mortgage. Not to mention the fact that you and your sister are always telling me I can't cook."

The humor did not work as it usually did. Hilary put the laundry basket down, sat on the bed, and looked closely at her son. He was so much like his father it almost hurt to study him.

"I want to understand what's going on, Chad, so why don't you tell me what this is *really* about?" Hilary's voice was soft and coaxing, and it surprised her to see tears fill her son's eyes.

"The baseball camp-out is only three weeks away." His whisper was tortured. "I'm the only one on the team who doesn't have a dad to go with him."

Hilary nodded and hoped he couldn't tell how tormented she was inside. They were both on the verge of sobbing, and for a moment she weighed the need for such a release. Praying swiftly, she decided against it at this time and then used some levelheaded logic to rescue them both.

"Will you allow me to look at this rationally?"

Chad nodded, and Hilary continued in a kind tone.

"If I were to meet a man this very moment and think he was the one, three weeks is hardly enough time to get married and get him on that camp-out with you."

Hilary waited for Chad to nod again. "I do want to marry again if God has someone for me. And I do want him to be a man who will love you and Lisa and want to do special things with you. But for now, I think we'd better leave this with my assuring you that I will try harder, or at least be praying more often about a mate.

"Why don't I phone your Uncle Jack tonight," she concluded. "Maybe he's free that weekend."

It was not exactly what Chad had wanted to hear, but Hilary could see he was beginning to accept the situation. Uncle Jack was a lot of fun, but as a pilot for a major airline, his weekends were rarely free.

Chad gave a final nod, hauled himself out of the chair, picked up the laundry basket, and preceded his mother out of the bedroom. The simple gesture was so like what his father would have done that Hilary felt on shaky ground all over again.

"What's wrong?" 16-year-old Lisa wanted to know as soon as her mother entered the kitchen. "Has Chad been on a father kick again?"

"Mind your own business, Lisa!" Chad grumbled to his sister.

"All right," Hilary cut in. "Let's not start something right now. There is laundry to be done and grass to be mowed. That leaves no time for arguing."

Chad started the washing machine, and Lisa went to the garage for the lawn mower. Hilary stood at the kitchen window but didn't focus on anything in particular.

It's been four years, Lord, her heart prayed. *Help us to wait on You. Help us to trust. And right now, please touch Chad's hurting heart.*

❧ ❧ ❧

"I'm just really trusting the Lord for this, Dad; in fact, my Bible study group is praying for you."

Adam Maxwell stared at his 25-year-old son with horror. "That was a joke just now, wasn't it, Brad?"

"No. You need a wife, and I've asked the guys to pray with me about that."

"I don't want another wife." Adam's voice was calm, even as his insides squirmed with embarrassment over his son's disclosure.

"Dad—" Brad's voice was as calm as his father's. "Greg is in his senior year, and I've been offered a job in Florida. We're not going to be home forever and—"

"Florida?" Adam sounded pleased. "You didn't tell me that. When do they—"

"You're changing the subject. Greg and I are not going to be around forever." Brad stopped when he saw a look of total confusion cross his father's face. His voice was gentle as he went on. "Mom's been dead for a long time, Dad, and you've never complained or been bitter. You learned to cook, clean, and even sew, but you need someone, someone to—"

"There are women at church," Adam cut him off, as though this explained everything.

"Dad, I love our church, but it's so big that the president could be sitting in the pew in front of you, and you wouldn't even meet him."

Brad turned away, and Adam watched as the younger man's hand covered his eyes.

He's choked up over this, Adam thought in amazement. He would have spoken, but Brad went on without turning.

"Greg met someone special a few weeks ago, and as I'm sure you've noticed, I'm very serious about Jenny." Brad finally turned, his eyes suspiciously wet. "Our leaving for college was only the first step to an empty nest. Greg graduates in a few months, and I'm probably moving out of the state. We want you to have someone to take care of you, someone who would love you as we do."

Now it was Adam's turn to be choked up, and he couldn't speak, even though Brad was waiting for some type of answer.

"I guess I've said enough," Brad said in a resigned voice. "She doesn't have to be the woman of your dreams, Dad—just someone you care about and who cares for you. Will you at least think about it?"

"Sure," Adam returned, finally able to speak.

"I've kept you too long," Brad continued. "You'll be late for practice."

"Right," Adam acknowledged, glad to be rescued. He picked up his hat and the equipment bag from the kitchen table and headed out the door. Not until he was behind the wheel of his van did he realize that he and Brad had not parted very well. It was tempting to go back and hug him, to let Brad know he appreciated his caring, but he was already late.

She doesn't have to be the woman of your dreams had been Brad's words. Adam couldn't stop the sad smile that crossed his face as he pulled up next to the baseball diamond.

She couldn't possibly be the woman of my dreams, son. That woman has been dead for ten years.

🌿 🌿 🌿

"Hey, Chad," Coach Maxwell called to his youngest player as he readied to leave the field.

Chad, who would normally have been thrilled to be singled out, hesitated before moving back to the bench where Adam sat with his notebook.

"Yeah, Coach?" the boy said, trying to smile.

"I just wanted to check with you about the camp-out. I don't have your money yet. Is there a problem?"

"Well, not really, but I don't know if I can go. You see, my dad's pretty busy, and I just don't know if we can fit it into our schedule."

Adam had to fight to keep his anger concealed. This boy was so obviously protecting his father, a father who probably didn't deserve that protection, Adam figured. Didn't these men know how much their sons needed attention?

"Well, you see what you can do. I need the money next week, okay?"

"Sure. Thanks, Coach." Trotting in the direction of his bicycle before the older man could say another word, Chad told himself he had one week to come up with a good excuse.

❧ ❧ ❧

Adam sat in his van outside the Farrell house, feeling surprised at its shabbiness. As soon as Chad had spoken of his father's busy schedule, Adam's mind had conjured up a picture of a wealthy, fast-moving businessman with little time for home and family. By the time Adam reached the front door, however, he'd decided that the man Chad was protecting must be a bum.

"I'll get it," Lisa called to the household in general when the bell rang. She had never met Chad's coach, so the man beyond the threshold was a stranger to her.

"Hello," he said briefly, "I'm Adam Maxwell, Chad's baseball coach. May I please speak to your father?"

"My father?" Lisa sounded uncertain, and Adam could have kicked himself. Chad's parents must be divorced. Why hadn't he realized that before?

"My mother is here," Lisa offered in the uncomfortable silence.

Adam smiled at her understanding. "May I please speak with her?"

"Sure." Lisa held the door wide, and Adam stepped into the living room. The interior was clean but as worn as the exterior, and Adam felt a wave of compassion for Chad. He watched the attractive young woman who had opened the door disappear into another room. Adam turned to take in the entire room, and so was unprepared when he looked back to see Chad's mother. He realized in an instant that even if he had watched her come into the room, he would not have been prepared.

Vulnerable. It was the first word that popped into his head at the sight of her small form and huge brown eyes. He knew from the hesitant look in her eye that he'd have to tread lightly.

"I'm sorry to bother you, Mrs. Farrell. I'd really hoped to see your husband about the camp-out."

Chad entered the room at that moment, so Adam missed the surprised look in Hilary's eyes.

"It's really not my practice to interfere, but this team camp-out means a lot to the boys, and Chad said his father was too busy to attend. I came today to encourage your husband to join us. We always have a great time, and like I said, it means so much to the boys."

Adam stopped when an unreadable look came over his hostess' face. He watched Hilary give her son a long, loving look before turning back to him and speaking with great compassion.

"Chad is usually a very honest boy. In fact, there have been so few lies that I can tell you every time he has lied to me in 13 years. When he does lie, he does it to protect himself."

Adam felt as though he'd come into the third act of a bad play, but he watched as Hilary turned to her son once again.

"I really do understand," she said to him, "but you owe your coach an explanation."

When Chad's eyes met Adam's, they were filled with tears. "I'm sorry I lied about my dad, Coach. My dad's dead. We called my uncle to see if he could take me, but he said he had to work that weekend. I don't know why I didn't tell you, except that I'm the only kid on the team who doesn't have a dad."

Adam's heart broke just a little over this admission, and he responded quietly. "Thank you for telling me the truth, Chad. As it is, you're not the only boy whose father cannot attend."

"I'm not?" Chad was genuinely surprised.

"No. There are three others. One does bring his uncle, but the other two come as my boys. I have a large tent, so I'll just plan on having three boys this year."

"Really?" Chad's eyes were full of wonder. This was better than Uncle Jack.

"Really." Adam's smile grew large at the boy's look of delight. "I'll get out of your way now," he said to Hilary while moving toward the door.

"Thank you," she said softly as he was on his way out.

Adam looked at her and realized they hadn't even been introduced. "By the way, I'm Adam Maxwell."

Hilary took his outstretched hand. "I'm Hilary Farrell," she responded with a smile.

"Are you by any chance free for dinner this coming week?" Adam would wonder for days where that question had come from, but it was too late now.

"Oh, well, I'm, that is—"

"That means yes," Chad cut in from somewhere over her shoulder.

"Great." Adam's smile had become very amused. "I'll pick you up on Thursday, seven o'clock."

Hilary shut the door in a state of shock.

"It's just a date, Mom." Lisa's logical voice drifted through her fog. "He didn't ask you to marry him."

"But he might," Chad interjected.

"Be quiet, Chad," his sister told him, "and come into the kitchen with me."

❧ ❧ ❧

"Stop grinning at me, Brad."

"I can't help it. If you could see how many times you've straightened your tie, you'd know what I find so amusing."

"Don't you have something else to do?" Adam growled.

Brad took himself off, but not before he smelled his father's aftershave and whistled appreciatively. Adam sat down on the edge of the bed when he'd gone.

What have I done, Lord? I don't even know this woman. I mean, I've seen Chad at church, so I assume she's a believer, but I'm not sure. What is it about her that I can't get out of my mind? Adam continued to pray, committing himself and the evening to the Lord, and then realized the time was getting away. He picked up his keys, unsure of what the evening would bring but determined not to be late.

☙ ☙ ☙

"If a band of gypsies came along right now and wanted to buy you, Chad Farrell, I'd sell. I can't believe you got me into this. What if he's an ax murderer?"

"He's my coach, Mom," Chad told her reasonably from his place on her bed. "I don't think he's ever murdered anyone."

Hilary didn't hear him; she was back in her closet changing her blouse for the fifth time. Not that she had that many blouses from which to choose—she'd put on the blue one three times and the red one twice.

It was hot, so she opted for lightweight white summer pants and sandals. The only question that remained was which top to wear with the pants. She'd decided on the blue, and was in the bathroom working on her hair when the doorbell rang. When she was done, she moved from her bedroom to the dining room and set her purse on the table. She knew she should wait for Adam in the living room, but she couldn't make herself go that far.

Lisa found her just after Chad joined her from the bedroom, telling her softly that her date had arrived.

"He's here, Mom." She sounded apologetic.

"I didn't hear the doorbell!" Hilary announced as though it was the most important oversight of the evening.

"He's wearing a suit," Lisa said softly and watched her mother freeze.

"Oh, no! Please, Chad," Hilary whispered furiously. "Please tell him I can't go. Please—"

Hilary stopped when Adam appeared in the doorway. He could tell something was wrong by the look on Lisa's face, and though he knew it was presumptuous of him to leave the living room, he'd come to tell Hilary that if she'd rather not go, it was fine with him. One look at her sweet, vulnerable face, however, and he changed his mind.

Hilary watched his eyes skim over her before he stepped into the room. He took her hand in his and moved back toward the door.

"We'll see you guys later," he called over her shoulder, and Hilary had no choice but to follow. Lisa spotted her mother's purse as they were headed out the door and ran to press it into her hand. Lisa and Chad watched from the front door for just a moment and then closed it, thinking the two adults didn't need an audience.

Adam held the van door open for his date, but Hilary hesitated. "I'm sorry about the way I'm dressed. If you'd rather we cancel tonight, I'll understand. I know you must be busy."

"You're right, I am busy. Tonight I have a date with Hilary Farrell. If you'll get in, we'll pop back over to my place, I'll change into something more casual, and then we'll go to this great Italian restaurant across town. The food is wonderful, but the atmosphere is casual. Do you like Italian?"

Hilary could only nod as she climbed into the van. The ride to Adam's house was quiet, but when they pulled up before a lovely two-story, Hilary began to babble.

"I'll just wait here for you. I don't mind, and I'm sure I'll be in the way if I come in."

Adam waited until she was through. "My son is here. Why don't you come inside and meet him?"

"Oh! All right." Hilary wondered how many more times she would make a fool of herself this evening.

"Brad, this is Hilary Farrell," Adam said a few minutes later. "Hilary, this is my son, Brad. Have a seat, and I'll be back in a few minutes."

Hilary sat in the first chair she came to and tried to calm the frantic beating of her heart. The house was lovely, she observed, and as she let her gaze roam the room, her eyes rested on the portrait of a beautiful woman over the mantel. She glanced at Adam's son and found him watching her.

"My mother," Brad told her simply, and for some reason, Hilary relaxed.

"How long has she been gone?"

"Over ten years. I understand you're widowed yourself."

Hilary nodded. "Four years now, but sometimes it feels like a lifetime." Hilary let herself lean back in the chair, crossing her legs gracefully. Her eyes were once again taking in the room, a room that gave evidence to the fact that there had been no lack of funds for this family.

"It's hard when the breadwinner dies, especially if the wife isn't trained in any particular field." She smiled suddenly at the nice-looking young man across from her. "But we make it work; God always provides."

"I quite agree with you there," Brad replied and found himself the recipient of one of Hilary's beautiful smiles. He watched her tense again when his father returned. He thought of the phrase "abandoned kitten" and decided that she gave new meaning to the words. He found himself praying as they left that she would relax with his dad and find out what a great guy he was.

❧ ❧ ❧

"Dessert?"

"I couldn't," Hilary told him in all honesty. It had been years since she'd had such a big meal. The bread sticks had come nonstop, and before the entree, a salad had been delivered that was large enough to feed an entire family. Lasagna was the main course, and even though it was Hilary's favorite, she'd struggled to get through her portion.

"How about some coffee?"

"Please," Hilary told him with a smile and waited quietly as he ordered.

"What do you do for a living?" she asked when the waitress had left their table. During the meal they'd talked about their children and various other topics, but by unspoken agreement had never let the conversation range to subjects more personal.

"I'm a mathematics professor at the university."

Hilary was silent for a few seconds. "Math was my worst subject," she finally admitted, certain now that they had nothing in common.

"Some of my students could say the same thing." Adam replied dryly.

Hilary laughed and then answered when Adam returned the question. He noticed that she moved her hands from the tabletop to her lap before she replied.

"I clean houses."

"Oh," Adam looked genuinely interested. "How often?"

"I don't work the weekends, but I have seven houses that I clean every week."

"Seven?" he exclaimed softly. "You actually clean more than one a day?"

"On Tuesdays and Thursdays I do. They're smaller than my other houses; in fact, one is an apartment."

Adam nodded, and both were relieved when the coffee arrived. The rest of the meal was strained, and neither one knew exactly why.

Hilary rescued them both by admitting that she had to be up early in the morning and should get home. Adam was more than happy to comply, and the drive to her house was made in almost complete silence.

The strain did not lift, not even when he walked her to the door and said goodbye. Hilary found herself hoping that she could make herself scarce when he came a few weeks later to take Chad camping.

🌿 🌿 🌿

Adam lay in his sleeping bag and listened to the sound of the boys as they slept. After the way they'd hiked in on foot, made camp, and helped with supper, it wasn't any wonder that they were dead to the world. Talk around the campfire had been brief, but not brief enough.

The conversation on summer vacation plans had started out innocently but had taken an unexpected turn when one of the fathers suggested that everyone tell his family vacation plans. Chad had been the seventh to share, saying honestly that his family didn't go on vacation.

Adam had waited then for some of the other boys to admit the same thing, but whether they all really did have plans or had simply made them up, it didn't matter. Out of 15 boys, Chad Farrell was the only team member whose family had nothing special planned for that summer. Adam had questioned him when they had a moment alone.

"No vacation, huh, Chad?"

"No," he said softly. "Mom can't get the days together."

"What do you mean?"

"Well," he explained, his voice matter-of-fact. "She tries to work it out so she has days off in the same week, but they always need her. But," Chad's face brightened as he added, "she does have two weekdays right together in June—Thursday and Friday—so we'll have a four-day weekend."

"Where will you go?"

"Go?" Chad looked momentarily confused. "Oh," his face suddenly cleared. "We can't afford to go anywhere, but we might see a movie on that Friday."

"What about your grandparents, Chad? Do you ever visit them?"

"No. Mom's parents are dead, and Grandpa and Grandma Farrell haven't been around much since Dad died."

Adam had reached and touched Chad's head in a tender gesture. The boy had grinned at him in sincere affection before heading off to find the other boys. Adam had stared after him in amazement. He'd never known such an unspoiled child.

Now, some hours later, Adam lay thinking of all he'd seen and heard about the Farrell family. Even as he was drifting off to sleep, his mind was forming a plan.

🌺 🌺 🌺

Hilary looked across her living room at Adam Maxwell and tried not to think about how good he looked in white tennis shorts and a dark green shirt. He'd been in her thoughts way too often since their date, and she knew that was going to have to stop. Hilary pulled her mind back to the present.

"Brad and I go every summer, and this time we want you to join us."

"I'm sure Chad would love it, but I'd have to talk with Lisa."

"Talk with me about what?" Lisa questioned as she came into the room, a half-eaten apple in her hand. Watching her, Adam knew a great rush of satisfaction. He'd prayed that the kids would be around when he arrived, because he knew he'd never persuade Hilary otherwise.

"Mr. Maxwell wants—"

"Adam," he corrected, and Hilary started again.

"Adam wants you and Chad to go on a camping trip with him—"

"No, Hilary," Adam broke in once more. "I want all *three* of you to go camping with Brad and me."

Hilary stared at him in total disbelief.

"We don't have a tent," she finally mumbled.

"I have everything you'll need—tents, sleeping bags, provisions—everything."

"Everything for what?" Chad asked as he joined the group, and Hilary nearly groaned. Instead, she listened in silence as Adam explained, then watched with something akin to horror as the excitement on her children's faces grew. She had dreamed of taking the kids on a trip, but camping? It had never crossed her mind.

She was a little amazed to hear herself agreeing and sat in stunned silence as Chad nearly danced around the room. Her eyes swung to Lisa to find her daughter's eyes sparkling with glee before she briefly met Adam's look. His tender smile made her face warm. It was several moments before she remembered her manners and finally offered coffee to her guest.

🌿 🌿 🌿

"You're sure you don't mind their joining us?" Adam asked Brad for the third time. Brad only grinned at his father and continued to load the van.

Adam wished he shared Brad's optimism. He'd thought long and hard about this trip and really felt he'd done the right thing, but doubts surfaced the moment he'd left the Farrells.

Maybe this trip would act as a purge. Hilary had constantly been in his thoughts for weeks now, and he told himself that if he could only get to know her, and she him, then maybe he could get her out of his system.

With this rather gloomy thought in mind, they were underway. It took just minutes for the van to pull up in front of the Farrell house, and 20 minutes later, both families were headed for the mountains.

❧ ❧ ❧

Hilary sat by the campfire and watched Lisa, flashlight in hand, walk toward the women's bathhouse. Brad had gone with Chad to the men's room, and Hilary wondered if she should have accompanied her daughter.

"She'll be fine." Adam read her look. "I picked this campground because it has such a family atmosphere and it's beautiful."

Hilary let her head fall back and take in the blanket of stars above. It was beautiful. No wonder Chad had been so excited.

"This is where you came with the boys, isn't it?" Hilary looked at him and watched him smile.

"Not exactly. We came to this area, but I don't think you would have cared for that trip. We hiked for several hours before we made camp, and since we were so far in, there were no bathing facilities of any kind."

Hilary's eyes had grown quite round, and Adam laughed. Anything either one of them might have said was cut short by the boys' arrival. Lisa was close on their heels, and within minutes they were roasting marshmallows and telling stories. A few hours later Adam suggested bed.

"We've got a long day of hiking and swimming tomorrow, so we're going to need our rest."

"Just think," Chad spoke as he made his way to the men's tent. "This is only Wednesday night, and we've still got four days to go."

Smiling at Brad and Adam across the fire, Hilary stood, retrieved her towel, toothbrush, and soap, and made her way to the women's shower room.

☙ ☙ ☙

"You never said anything to me about cutting up dead fish, Adam Maxwell!"

Adam hid a smile at Hilary's look of horror and shrugged. "Didn't your husband fish?"

"Yes, he did," she told him, still frowning fiercely. "But he always cleaned the fish himself. Did *your* wife clean the fish you caught?"

"No," Adam said with a grin, "but on the off chance that you'd just love to, I had to ask."

Hilary laughed and tried to put the fishnet over his head. Adam snatched it away from her, and they smiled at each other. Adam's look grew very tender as he took in her sunburned nose, and Hilary blushed. She transferred her gaze to the water below them and spoke wistfully.

"It's hard to believe we go home tomorrow, but I praise God for the time we've had. I don't know if I've thanked you properly, Adam, but you've given us a wonderful vacation."

Adam found he couldn't speak as he watched her adorable profile. He thought of how poorly his purge had worked. She was going to be someone whose faith was fake, but it hadn't been so. She was going to be someone who was grouchy at breakfast and a poor sport about the heat or mosquitoes. But she'd been none of those things. In less than 72 hours, this sweet, caring woman was more fully embedded in his thoughts than Adam believed possible.

"Hilary," Adam said suddenly, then waited for her face to turn to him. "If I asked you on a date once we were home, would you go?"

"Yes," she answered him softly and without hesitation. "Do you think you'll ask?"

His head moved affirmatively as he held her eyes with his own. He extended his hand in a careful gesture, his fingers reaching for hers. Hilary's hand went out and was captured within his own. No words were spoken; no words were needed.

Brad had told him that she need not be the woman of his dreams. Adam smiled to himself, looking forward to telling him just how wrong he'd been.

A Note from Lori: *Although I'm not specific in this story, I pictured the campground at Emerald Bay as I wrote. The campground is on Lake Tahoe, one of my favorite places. We camped there several times when I was a child and even as a teenager. The memories of my father, who was very good at driving and setting up our travel trailer, along with my mother, brother, cousins, aunt, and even a friend who joined us one time, are sweet beyond description.*

The Christmas Gift

"Why do you seek the living One among the dead?
He is not here, but He has risen."
Luke 24:5,6

Snow drifted past the kitchen window in a timely fashion, putting a clean dusting of powder on the previously fallen inches. There was no wind this December morning, and the large flakes dropped so straight to the ground that it looked as if someone had plumbed a line between the sky and earth.

Maggie Hartman came into the kitchen that moment and took a second to watch her foster daughter, who stood motionless at the window. Brenda stood with her nose pressed to the glass, anxiously watching the figure at work on the brick walkway, a snow shovel in his hands.

Brenda's mouse brown hair hung in a perfect line down to her slim shoulders. Maggie didn't need to see Brenda's tiny ears in order to picture the large hearing aids that rested in each. She also knew that if the little ten-year-old girl turned around, she would regard her out of eyes covered with bottle-thick lenses.

"I don't think we're going to go," the little girl finally said, having known Maggie was there all along.

"You'll go," Maggie said soothingly and moved farther into the room. "It's not supposed to snow that long, and Gary left the truck for you and Mark."

Maggie smiled to herself when she heard Brenda sigh. She could well remember the disappointments over the years when outings were canceled because of the weather, but it was different for Brenda. Brenda's entire life had been a disappointment, making something as simple as a canceled shopping trip more than a little upsetting.

Maggie had just poured herself a cup of coffee when her 23-year-old son, Mark, came in the back door.

"Well, the walk is clear, but I'm not sure how long it will last."

"Thank you, Mark. At least if the women come soon enough they can get in for Bible study."

"Are you ready to go, Brenda?" Mark wanted to know.

"We're still going to shop?" She regarded her large foster brother with anxious eyes.

"Of course. The roads don't look bad at all. Get your things, and we'll get out of here."

Brenda took time to smile hugely at Maggie before running for the back hall that held her coat, hat, and mittens.

It was now Maggie's turn to stand at the window as she watched the dark blue truck move down the street.

Brenda had originally come home with Gary in that very truck. In Gary's line of work as a social worker it would have been easy to bring a different child home each night. Maggie knew if she'd been in his place, the house would be full of these abused and abandoned children. But early on they had set up a policy, and Gary had never brought anyone home. Until Brenda.

When she arrived at the house in May, she weighed 42 pounds. Maggie had never seen such an emaciated child. Brenda's first nine and a half years of life had been spent with an often drunk, abusive father—one who hadn't bothered to feed her very often. Prior to coming to live with them, Brenda had never been to school, but it wouldn't have mattered. Her eyes had been so severely damaged by the abuse that she couldn't have read a book if she'd tried. And that wasn't all. She could barely hear Gary and Maggie before the aids were purchased.

The summer was more than half over before all the doctor appointments ended and a judge ruled that Brenda was to live with Gary and Maggie for the time being. Maggie recalled that day as one of the happiest of her life. She had not been able to have children after Mark was born, and it mattered not in the least that this child was not of her body. It didn't even matter that it might be temporary. For the time being Brenda was theirs, and Maggie was going to make the best of it.

Standing at the window, she now prayed, asking God with all her heart to bless Mark and Brenda that day. She couldn't say what exactly she was hoping for, but she asked for a blessing anyway, content to leave Brenda and Mark in God's hands.

❧ ❧ ❧

The occupants of the truck were fairly quiet as they made their way to the shopping mall. Brenda was tightly belted in, her eyes on the road, and her small 101 Dalmatians purse held closely in her hand. Mark glanced at her from time to time, but she didn't seem to notice.

"I have only six dollars," she told Mark for the second time.

"All right. Do you want to get something on your own or share a gift with me?"

"You would let me share a gift with you?" she said with some wonder.

"Of course. That's what big brothers are for."

Brenda didn't speak. She was not so young that she didn't know the truth. She would have given anything if Gary, Maggie, and Mark were her real family, but it simply wasn't so. And now that she could hear better, she understood that it was just a matter of time before she would be placed in permanent foster care.

Brenda didn't want such thoughts to ruin her time with Mark, so she made herself focus on other things, and they were parked and walking inside before she knew it.

"I think the bookstore first. Mom said Dad spotted a book on trains he'd like to have."

Brenda nodded and walked carefully beside him. The mall was noisy, and she was a little afraid of getting lost. Mark noticed her discomfort and would have gladly taken her hand, but he wasn't sure if she would welcome this. Brenda had come to live with his parents just two weeks after he'd left to take a job in Europe. He hadn't met her before five days ago and was still working at gauging what her facial expressions meant. He decided against taking her hand, but whenever they moved through a large crowd, his hand rested lightly on her shoulder.

Only 20 minutes passed before they were finishing up at the bookstore. They were at the checkout counter when Brenda said, "Here's my money."

"Well," Mark said, "since you have six dollars, why don't you just give me half of it?"

Brenda looked uncertain, but Mark counted out three of the bills and watched as she carefully tucked the others away.

Once out in the mall again Mark said, "Now Dad said something about a sweater for Mom."

"The pink one?"

"You know about the sweater?" Mark asked with surprised pleasure.

"I think so. She's looked at one in Crandell's three times."

"Let's go," Mark told her, and off they went. This time Brenda did tuck her hand into Mark's, and in record time they had made their purchases and headed to the food court for lunch. Mark had said a prayer for their meal, but even after he'd lifted his hamburger, Brenda sat still.

"What is it, Brenda? Don't you like burgers and fries?"

She stared at him for a moment and then asked quietly, "The sweater was more money than the book, wasn't it?"

Mark set his food aside. "Yes, it was, but that's not important because we're getting both of them what they want."

"I know, but I only gave you three dollars. Maybe you should tell Maggie that I only bought three dollars of her sweater."

"Now that's not a bad idea," Mark said with an exaggerated expression, eyes wide while one hand stroked his chin. "I'll put on the card that you bought the little pink buttons and the collar. What do you think?"

Brenda caught his teasing and smiled. She reached for a french fry, and for a time they ate in silence. Mark wanted to get to know her better, and after a moment asked gently, "How do you like living with Dad and Mom?"

"I like it. They're nice."

"They like you too."

Brenda didn't smile or reply.

"What did I say that's making you look worried?"

Brenda gave a little shrug. "I was just wondering where I'll live next."

"Would you like to go back with your dad?"

Brenda shook her head no, her eyes very serious behind her thick glasses. "He didn't like me, and I never got to go to school."

"What do you like most about school?"

"The Bible stories."

Mark nodded with satisfaction. He knew his parents had debated long and hard about where to send

Brenda to school. Mark looked forward to telling them that the Christian school had been the best choice.

"Do you have a favorite Bible character?"

"Daniel," she told him without hesitation. "He wasn't afraid."

"Do you get scared at times?"

Brenda nodded. "I try not to, but I do. Maggie tells me to trust in God, but I'm not sure I can do that. If I could just see Him and talk to Him I might, but I keep thinking He's going to be like my father."

Mark nodded, his heart breaking a little. "I can see why you'd feel that way. I've thought a lot about God over the years. Shall I tell you what I think of Him?"

Brenda nodded, her mouth full.

"I think He is like a father, *my* father."

Brenda's french fry stopped halfway to her mouth as she stared at her lunch companion. Gary Hartman was the most wonderful person Brenda had ever known. He was strong and kind, and his eyes always smiled as they looked at her. She never thought that God might be like *him*. That would be wonderful, but could it be true?

"Did I upset you, Brenda?" Mark asked gently.

"No," she said, but her voice was low. She went on to eat, but her face looked troubled. Again Mark wished he knew her better.

"Have you made any friends at school?"

"Yes. I play with Tara sometimes. She lives pretty close."

"Tara Nolan?"

"Yes. I like her, but her family is around a lot, and sometimes I get a little nervous."

"What makes you nervous?"

"Her brothers are all pretty big."

"I'm big," Mark tried to reason with her.

"You're different."

Her face turned pink on these words, and Mark knew it was time for a change in subject. They talked about the plans to be alone on Christmas Eve, for the service at church, and their gift opening. The whole family would join them on Christmas day.

"You'll get to play with Johanna," Mark told her, and this brought a full smile to her face. Johanna was Mark's young cousin, and even though they lived a few hours apart, according to his mother's letters, the little girls were ecstatic whenever they saw each other.

When their trash had been thrown away, the two shoppers browsed through the mall, covering every inch of the Disney Store, and then made their way back to the truck. The snow had let up some, and the ride home was quiet. The two of them sequestered themselves in Mark's bedroom in order to wrap the gifts and then snuck into the family room to put them under the tree. Mark then made his way to the kitchen in search of something warm to drink, but Brenda lingered by the tree as she often did.

Set in the center, the gifts pushed off to one side, was a nativity set. Maggie had the wise men off to one side because she said they'd just started their journey and weren't there the night the Savior was born, but the shepherds were close, and so was a tiny black lamb, two white ones, and a donkey. Brenda knelt down now and picked up the tiny manger with the Christ child lying on the bed of straw. Questions raced through her mind, but no answers followed.

"Brenda," Maggie called from the kitchen. "Would you like some hot chocolate?"

"Coming," the little girl called and carefully replaced the manger. She stood and stared down at the scene for a few more minutes and, turning, she walked slowly toward the kitchen.

❧ ❧ ❧

"You're awfully quiet tonight," Gary commented as he handed a dripping plate to Brenda.

"I'm just thinking."

"About?"

"About God."

Gary stopped what he was doing. He let the next dish slide back beneath the suds and laid the dishcloth on the edge of the sink. He then turned, leaned against the counter, and looked at Brenda.

"And what did you decide?"

"I don't know. I never thought about God until I moved here, and then Maggie talked about Him like He was a father, and I thought He must be like my father."

"How do you feel about that?"

"I don't like it. My father is mean."

Gary stared at her, his heart praying. "Has something else happened?"

"Sort of. Mark said that he thought God was more like you, not like my father."

Gary took the plate and towel from her hands and set them aside. He then pulled two chairs from the table, keeping them close. Brenda took a seat, and Gary sat across from her, their knees touching.

"I have only met your father once, Brenda, so I don't know him very well, but I do know this—God the Father does not hurt His children; He loves them."

Brenda's look was almost defiant. "But He sent His Son away. He sent Him to earth and then to die."

Gary felt himself tremble. He loved this child as though she were his own, and very gently he reached and pulled her into his lap, praying as he did so—begging God, actually—to give him the words.

"If you could imagine the most wonderful father in the whole wide world, what would he be like?"

Brenda's ear lay against his chest, and she spoke with conviction.

"Well, he would be nice, and he wouldn't ever hit you when you didn't do anything wrong or put you in your room and leave you there."

"Anything else?"

Brenda now leaned forward and looked at him.

"He would take you places and make sure you had toys and clothes and stuff."

"What about your safety? Would he see to that?"

"What do you mean?"

"Well, say there was a car coming down the street that went out of control, and in order to save you, your father would have to die. Is that something a perfect father would do?"

Brenda bit her lip. "I'm not sure."

"Well, I want you to think about that, honey, because that's just what God did. In order to save us from our sin, He had to die. God the Son came to earth to be born and then grew to be a man in order to die for us. God's heaven is perfect, and a sinful man cannot get in on his own. He has to have a Savior."

"But it was so mean to send His Son away," Brenda tried to reason, and Gary took another tack.

"Whose house is this, Brenda?"

"Yours and Maggie's."

"That's right. Now if someone comes to our front door, should we let him in?"

"Well, that depends."

"On what?"

"On what he wants."

"So you think that Maggie and I should have the say?"

"Yes. It's your house."

"That's right." Gary's voice was very gentle now. "And heaven is God's home. He alone says who has the right to come into His home. Without Jesus Christ none of us could go, but He provided the way by dying on the cross. Did He have fun doing that? No, but God loved us so much that He had to find a way to bring us to Him. That way was Jesus Christ."

"How did Jesus feel about it?"

"Well . . ." This was a first for Gary so he took a moment to think. "I don't think He enjoyed it; in fact, I know He didn't, but He knew there was no other way, so He told His Father in heaven that He would do whatever God asked of Him. And do you know what, Brenda? He didn't just die for the sins that were committed right then, but for all the sins of all time. That's why we can come to Christ today, 2000 years later—

because He finished the job when He died and rose again on the third day."

"What do you mean He rose again?"

"He arose."

Brenda's brow lowered. She heard that and even sang it at Easter time, but it made no sense at all.

"I still don't know what that means."

Gary stared at her. How could she have missed that? He must have misunderstood her. "He didn't stay dead," Gary told her simply, not sure if this would clear things up. "He arose."

"He's a flower?"

"No, honey. He came back alive."

"But that's impossible, Gary. Dead is dead."

Gary licked his lips. He and Maggie had talked about this. Her teacher at school and at Sunday school had talked about this. How could she have missed the most important event in all of history?

"Jesus Christ is God, Brenda."

"Okay."

"You knew that?"

"Yes."

"Death can't keep God down, Brenda. They put Him in the grave and sealed the door with a huge rock, but no seal can keep God inside. He's God and *He* has the power over death. Nothing could keep God in the grave—not the huge rock or the soldiers waiting outside. He rose again. "Arose" means he came back to life."

"He arose," Brenda stated.

"That's right."

"I didn't know that word."

Gary smiled. "All this time you thought God sent His Son away from Him forever."

Brenda nodded. "But He didn't."

"No, He didn't."

Gary wasn't sure what to expect next, but Brenda's asking to be excused surprised him.

"Has our talk upset you, honey?"

"No. I just want to go to my room for a while."

"All right."

"Oh," Brenda's hand came to her mouth. "I forgot about the dishes."

"That's all right. I'll finish, but come and see me if you decide you want to talk."

"All right."

Gary hugged her as she slid off his lap and then sat quietly as she left the room. He was sitting very still some 20 minutes later when Maggie came looking for him. He held his hand out to her and she took Brenda's chair.

"Pray with me, Maggie. Pray that Brenda understands this time."

🌾 🌾 🌾

"I understand now," Brenda sat in her room and told God, "but I'm not too sure if I can do what Gary and Maggie have done. They live for You every day, and sometimes I forget You're even there. I don't mean to, but I do." Her little heart sighed very softly. "Last week Maggie had a headache, but she still had Bible study. I don't know if I can be so good like that all the time."

All at once the little girl ran out of things to say, and in that instant she remembered the words of her teacher, the ones about the way people try to wrap themselves up to look pretty, but they're not pretty inside. Brenda suddenly knew she was trying to do that.

"If you still want me," she whispered to God, "I'll do my best."

❧ ❧ ❧

Brenda's eyes were wide the night of the Christmas Eve service, and Gary, Maggie, and Mark all noticed her awestruck expression. She was quieter than usual, but there was also a special serenity about her. She stood in wonder over the service, the singing, and the candles, and then nearly trembled with excitement when it was time to go home and open gifts.

It was a wonderful evening, full of love and surprises. Gary loved his book, and Maggie's eyes shone when she saw the sweater. Mark and Brenda shared conspiratorial looks when they watched her hold the soft yarn to her cheek.

An hour later, the floor littered with boxes, bows, and wrap, Mark pressed a small gift into his mother's hand.

"I thought you gave me a gift."

"Well," he smiled. "This is just one more."

She weighed it a moment and then laughed.

"I think it's empty."

"You'll have to open it to find out."

Maggie smiled at him and picked at the tape. Inside was a business card with Mark's name on it. Maggie studied it, looked to her husband, and then looked back at Mark.

"Is this one of your old ones, dear? It has a Minnesota address."

As soon as the words were out of her mouth, she understood.

"Oh, Mark." Tears flooded her eyes, and Gary jumped up from her side to go to his boy. He wrapped his arms around him, and when he broke away, his eyes were suspiciously moist.

"February," Mark told them with a beaming smile. "I'll have to go back to Europe for about a month, but then it's a permanent move to this office."

There were hugs all around as Brenda joined in the fun, delighted that Mark would not be going away for good. The next few minutes were spent cleaning the floor. All papers were checked so that nothing of value would be thrown away.

"It sure is a lot of paper," Brenda commented.

"Yes, it is," Gary agreed, "and now that reminds me." He reached into his breast pocket, as though he'd really forgotten, and pulled out a piece of paper. "I have one more gift for you."

Brenda was unaware of the way both Maggie and Mark had stopped what they were doing in order to watch the scene.

"This is for me?" She looked at the folded paper.

"Yes," Gary told her.

Brenda opened it, the eyes behind the lenses very serious. She studied the official looking document, but then looked to Gary.

"What is it?"

"Well, you don't have to read it. I'll just tell you that it says that Brenda May Small is now Brenda May

Hartman, and that her parents are Gary and Maggie Hartman."

Brenda's little mouth fell open. "For real?"

"For real," Gary told her, his eyes flooding with tears.

"You're my dad now?"

"I'm your dad now."

Brenda flew into his arms, and Gary cried unashamedly against her little shoulder. She was still so frail, and he had admitted to God that it would be the hardest thing he'd ever done if he'd been asked to let her go.

From Gary's arms she went to Maggie, who held her close for a long time, her own heart so full she couldn't speak. At last Mark hugged her.

"That makes you my brother," Brenda told him, her face alight.

"Yes, it does." He barely managed the words.

"For real."

"For real," he agreed as he gently kissed her brow.

They sat up much too late, eating popcorn and watching *White Christmas*, and it was a very sleepy daughter that Gary carried off to bed. He was tucking her gently under the covers, expecting her to remove her glasses and hearing aids so he could lay them on the nightstand, when she took his hand.

"I had another present too, Gary," she said softly. "But I didn't have a paper."

"Oh? What was it?"

"It was a talk present."

"You wanted to tell us something?"

Brenda's head nodded against the pillow.

"Can you tell me now?"

"After we talked that night, I told God that if He still wanted me, I would do my best. And then tonight during the service, I thanked God that Jesus died for my sins. Did I do all right, Gary? Did I believe all right?"

"Oh, Brenda." Gary was overcome and could only gather her back into his arms.

"I love you, Gary," she whispered close to his ear, "and I love it that God is just like you."

Gary didn't try to correct her. There would be time. She knew now; she understood. Her little heart had opened up to the truth, and just as she now belonged to Gary and Maggie, she was God's child as well. Mark's move back to the states and Brenda's becoming their daughter were gifts beyond price, but when a man was able to take his children into eternity with him— this was the greatest Christmas gift of all.

A Note from Lori: *I never know how characters are going to affect me before I start writing about them, so each one is a surprise. I had Brenda in my mind for a long time, and I knew she would be special, but if I may be honest with you: She completely melts my heart. No matter how many times I read this story, I am filled with emotion and tears that I can't stem. I love Brenda's innocence and honesty. I love it that when she learned all the facts, she knew the only thing left to do was to trust in Jesus Christ. May we all be so trusting and ready to open our hearts to the Lord.*

The Rancher's Lady

*For I am confident of this very thing,
that He who began a good work in you
will perfect it until the day of Christ Jesus.*

Philippians 1:6

Shasta McGregor, dressed in well-worn jeans, boots, and a light cotton shirt, stepped down from the cab of the truck and followed her boss, Morgan Clark, into the largest saddle shop in Brisbane, Australia.

"I think you need a change," Morgan told her, continuing the conversation that had begun in the truck.

"I changed just before we left the ranch," Shasta told him dryly, ignoring his real meaning.

"I want you to leave Burbarra."

Shasta's wry humor fled, and she stopped in an aisle filled with horse blankets and various tack, forcing Morgan to stop with her. His gray head was turned in her direction, and for a moment Shasta couldn't say anything. Leave Burbarra? Could he be serious? Morgan owned Burbarra, a huge sheep ranch outside of Dalby and her home for the last 11 years.

"You're firing me?"

"No," he said gently, wishing his wife, Peg, had accompanied them. "I'm suggesting some time away. You're thin and pale, and I think it stems from a fear that you're going to run into Frank and DeeDee every Sunday at church or each time we come into town. I saw the way you tensed when that green Ford truck went by, and it wasn't even Frank's. If you left here, you wouldn't have that anxiety."

"Leave Burbarra?"

"Not just Burbarra," he said quietly, his eyes watching her carefully. "Australia."

Again Shasta stared at him before saying very slowly, "And just where, Morgan, do you suggest I go?"

"California," her boss replied without a moment's hesitation.

"*The United States!*" Shasta exclaimed in horror, staring at Morgan as if he'd taken leave of his senses.

Morgan's mouth tugged into a smile. "Come now, Shasta, it's not Outer Mongolia."

"It might as well be," Shasta said with a shake of her blonde head, and for a time they dropped that particular topic of conversation.

Morgan's supplies were being loaded into the rear of the truck when Shasta asked, "Why California?"

"Because I have a mate there. He runs several cattle ranches, one of which doubles as a vacation ranch during the summer months. I know he would value a rider with your experience and way with people."

"I'm not interested," Shasta told him flatly, and Morgan let it go.

They made several more stops: Morgan went to the barber, and Shasta worked at filling a list Peg had sent with her. After a late lunch, they were back on the road to Burbarra. Morgan had not referred to California since they left the saddle shop, but knowing they would be in the truck for hours, he no longer hesitated.

"I think you should consider it."

Shasta didn't feign ignorance. "Oh, Morgan," she spoke softly. "I can't imagine leaving here. This year has been painful enough without adding a separation to my load."

Morgan had no immediate answer to this, so they both fell silent, their minds reflecting back to last December and this February.

Just before Christmas, Frank Iverson, a wonderful Christian man Shasta had been seeing for more than a year, asked her to be his wife. Believing for many months that this was the man God had willed for her, Shasta had accepted with a joyful heart.

However, in February, not even two months later, a woman Frank had not seen in ten years moved back into the area. Shasta had not been worried; after all, she and Frank loved each other and were scheduled to be married on July 29. But Shasta had been wrong. Frank had come to her at the end of February and said that seeing DeeDee Wharton again had changed everything. He said that it would be a lie for him to pretend that nothing was wrong. He could not marry Shasta when his feelings had changed so much.

Shasta had not begged him to reconsider or lashed
out in anger. She just quietly returned the ring. A
month later, at the end of March, Frank and DeeDee
were married in a very private ceremony. It was now the
end of April, and Shasta still thought about Frank all
day, every day. There was no bitterness in her heart, but
Morgan was right, she was hurting in a way that felt
akin to mourning and thought she would continue to
do so for many months.

"Let me give him a call, Shasta."

"Who?" This time she didn't really know.

"Kyle Harrington, the man who owns and runs the
Harrington Cattle Company. His vacation ranch is in
Fort Ross, right off the Pacific coast. Peg and I were
there years ago. It's a beautiful spot, and I think a job
there for the summer might act as a type of balm for
the hurt you're feeling."

Shasta opened her mouth to protest yet again, but
Morgan forestalled her with a gentle hand on her arm.

"Just think about it, Shasta, and do some praying.
Peg and I are not trying to push you away. In fact, Peg
cried last night just at the thought of your leaving. I'm
suggesting this for you. Will you at least give it some
thought?"

"Yes," Shasta agreed quietly. She was a reasonable,
levelheaded woman, and besides that, she would do
just about anything for Morgan or Peg Clark.

The remainder of the ride home was uneventful,
but that suited Shasta very well. She had a great
amount of thinking to do, and quiet was just what she
needed.

❧ ❧ ❧

One month later a sober Peg stood next to Shasta at the Brisbane airport. Morgan had gone off to find some cups of tea. Peg had so much to say, but nothing would come.

Finally, "You will come back, won't you, Shasta?"

"You know I will," she said simply.

"I'll come after you if you don't." Peg tried to keep her voice light but couldn't quite manage it.

"Why wouldn't I, Peg?" Shasta shifted in her seat to look up at the older woman.

"Oh, Shasta," Peg nearly groaned. "You're a lovely girl who's lived in the outback for years. I despaired that you would even recognize an eligible male if you saw one. Then when one did come into your life, you fell headfirst into love, but he didn't know a good thing when he had it and broke your heart."

Shasta wasn't hurt by Peg's words. She thought she understood, but when she spoke, her voice was more than a little dubious concerning Peg's theory.

"Let me get this straight. You're sure that some American bloke is going to think I'm a walking dream and propose on the spot, and I'll never come back to Australia because I'll have stars in my eyes and forget where I'm from, right?"

Peg sighed. Her eyes searched the face of this young woman who was like a daughter to her. In so doing, she felt something clench around her heart. Shasta was lovely, but she'd never known it and never needed or tried to do anything to enhance it. Her dark blonde hair was thick and fell in a fat braid down her back. Wispy bangs sat gently against her brow. Technically her chin was too stubborn, but even that was redeemed by the largest pair of brown eyes Peg had ever seen and high cheekbones that were always a rosy pink.

"Just promise you'll return, Shasta," she managed at last. "At least for a visit. Say you'll come back."

Seeing how serious she really was, Shasta nodded and the women hugged. Morgan appeared with mugs of tea just minutes later, but no one could drink a drop. All too soon her flight was called, and the Clarks hugged their precious Shasta one last time. Feeling much younger than her 32 years, Shasta forced herself to walk away and not look back. She had prayed long and hard about this and felt a true peace, but a tiny corner of her heart couldn't help but wonder if she might be making the biggest mistake of her life.

🌹 🌹 🌹

Shasta had never been so disoriented in her whole life as she was when the huge Qantas airplane finally touched down at the San Francisco International Airport. She was feeling sick with exhaustion at the thought that she still had to go through customs. The service had been fine, and her seat had been comfortable, but who would have thought a flight could be so long?

Having been to baggage claim and through customs, her fine leather saddle seemed to weigh a ton, but she made herself push on, exiting the building to wait outside for the bus that would take her farther north.

With an effort she fought back tears of fatigue. She heaved her bag over one shoulder, her saddle over the other, and in less than 20 minutes was sitting aboard a large bus. She had seen only three miles' worth of sights in the San Francisco Bay area when she fell sound asleep, her head against the window.

Shasta didn't change buses until Santa Rosa. There was a bit of a wait, but her spirits perked up some when she had a strong cup of tea and saw that the bus would be delivering her out to the Fort Ross area around 4:00 P.M. Morgan had said she was expected on the twenty-sixth, and she thought it would give a poor impression to arrive a day late.

The ride out to the coast was wonderful. The landscape turned very hilly with scrub brush in all directions. Sheep and large lambs dotted the hillsides, and Shasta ached to get near them. The bus let her off about a mile from the ranch, and after Shasta had asked directions of the bus driver, she started out on foot. Her limbs were giving her trouble by the time she reached the gate that read Harrington Cattle Company, but knowing that a job and a hot meal would be waiting for her at the other end, she pushed on.

🌹 🌹 🌹

Kyle Harrington's head went back in agony as his fingers were smashed between the bull and the wall, but no words came from his mouth. He gasped slightly as he began to think that his newest hand, a young woman who had come highly recommended, had never been near a cattle ranch, let alone worked with large animals.

"The rope was pinching me," JoAnn whined when she saw his look of pain.

"Was it?" Kyle's voice was amazingly calm, but his fingers were still throbbing, and they still had not secured his largest bull. The animal was not vicious or wild, but he was huge, and it helped to have an extra hand.

"Yes. Are you hurt?" she asked belatedly.

"Yes," he admitted as the pain eased slightly, "but I'll live." He swung around and moved toward his foreman.

"Brian?"

"Yeah, boss."

"See what you can do with that bull. JoAnn can help you."

Brian gave him a long-suffering look, but Kyle ignored it and made his way from the barn area to the ranch office. His right hand was still throbbing, and he knew he had to put some distance between himself and JoAnn before he spoke with her about what he expected from his employees. He also needed to make a phone call to the hotel. He was halfway across the dirt expanse when he spotted a small blonde woman with a saddle and kit bag. He stopped when she spoke.

"Excuse me, could you tell me where I might find Mr. Harrington?"

"I'm Kyle Harrington," he said, his mind barely registering her accent.

Shasta smiled and put her hand out. Kyle forgot himself and offered his right one. Shasta had always enjoyed a firm handshake, and now that she was nervous, it was a

little stronger than usual. An odd look passed over Mr.
Harrington's face, but Shasta didn't catch it.

"I'm Shasta McGregor. I believe you're expecting
me."

Kyle studied her through his pain and was not
impressed. She was a tiny thing, built like JoAnn and
looking just as helpless. He also thought it rather presumptuous of her to bring her saddle.

"From Australia?"

"Yes. I hope I'm not too late."

"Hardly," Kyle said softly. "I was not expecting you
until the twenty-sixth."

Shasta blinked at him. "This is the twenty-sixth."

"No," he spoke slowly, "it's not. It's the twenty-fifth,
and I don't have time to speak to you until tomorrow.
You can come to my office at eight o'clock." He turned
and started away.

"Eight tomorrow morning?" Shasta said to his
retreating back.

Kyle turned back very slowly, all the while praying
that he would keep control of his emotions.

"Yes," he replied with a deliberate calm that sounded
just a bit menacing. "Eight tomorrow morning. Is there
some problem with that?"

There was every problem with it, but Shasta
shook her head no and watched him walk away. She
glanced around at the beautiful ranch house, office,
and barns but couldn't find it in her heart to appreciate any of them. How could she have gotten the
days mixed up?

Kyle Harrington was gone now, but Shasta found
herself staring at the door he'd disappeared through for

a moment longer. With a deep sigh, she hoisted her bag once again, her saddle now dangling from her hand. The driveway seemed twice as long on the way back down, but she went anyway. She'd had enough American currency to buy a bus ticket to Fort Ross but no more. What in the world was she going to do?

❧ ❧ ❧

Kyle's voice had been a study in gentleness, but JoAnn was in tears after five minutes' worth of consultation.

"I can't help it," she cried, "I've never done this type of work before."

Kyle's heart sank with dread, but his voice was still kind. "But you said you were experienced with ranch work."

"In the office," she sobbed. "I worked in the office at Sea Ranch. I've never been around cows or horses."

Kyle took in her pretty face and thick blonde hair and wondered how much of the recommendation had hinged on her looks. At the same time he handed JoAnn a box of tissues. She sobbed for several more minutes, and then Kyle, telling himself he had no one to blame since he'd allowed someone else to hire her, gently mapped out what he would be needing for the remainder of the summer.

JoAnn looked horrified at times, and Kyle couldn't help but wonder what she thought they did on a ranch. He told her that when the guests started arriving in just ten days, she would be handling some of them, but by now she seemed too upset to take it in. They were already late for supper, so Kyle let her go. He was hungry as well and very tired. He ate and went to bed without giving Shasta McGregor another thought.

☙ ☙ ☙

Shasta woke with a start and it took an instant for her to figure out why her back and neck ached. She felt the leather of her saddle under her cheek and finally understood. She sat up with a groan and looked down at her dusty clothes. Her first night in America had not gone the way she'd planned.

After leaving the ranch, she'd walked down the road for a time and then realized that even if she did walk back to the small town of Jenner, she hadn't money to buy a thing. With this in mind she began to look for a place to bed down for the night. There were many possibilities, and long before dark, Shasta was settled in behind a large rock that sheltered her from the wind. It wasn't the softest bed she'd ever had, but it would do.

She'd woken often in the night, but that was better than sleeping through and not being able to move at all in the morning. Each time she'd stirred, she forced herself to move around and stretch her limbs. By the time she slept for the last time she was feeling pretty good. However, it now felt as if she'd overslept. She tried to gauge the time by the sun but only felt disoriented. She realized then that she was still suffering from jet lag.

With a determined push she rose from the ground and gathered her gear. On rather stiff legs it took half an hour to gain the ranch, and already the sun was very hot. Shasta had taken time to comb her hair, but she knew she was dusty and sweaty and was not sure it had been worth the effort. Having no idea what time it actually was, she knocked on the door she'd seen Mr. Harrington enter the afternoon before.

☙ ☙ ☙

Brian stuck his head in the back door of Kyle's office and spoke quietly to his employer. "JoAnn's gone."

"She's what?"

"Gone. Told Marcy she didn't think she could do the job and that she was leaving. A car just came for her."

Kyle nodded, not knowing if he was pleased or not. She had not been a good employee, but he was now shorthanded. *Maybe I was shorthanded all along*, he thought ruefully.

Jean, his secretary, took that instant to poke her head in as well.

"Shasta McGregor is here to see you."

Kyle glanced at his watch and frowned. She was half an hour late. Didn't anyone take their work seriously these days?

"Send her in," he finally said.

Both Brian and Jean disappeared, and a moment later a small, rather dusty woman stood inside his office door.

"Please, sit down," Kyle instructed from where he stood behind his desk, and Shasta didn't miss the cool tone of his voice. She'd left her saddle and bag in the front office, but she had a thin portfolio with her, and from that she withdrew some papers.

"These are my references and resume." Shasta passed him the spotless papers and sat back, thinking he would want to read them. However, even after he took them from her hand, he continued studying her. Shasta licked her lips in a nervous gesture and waited. It didn't take long.

"I might as well tell you up front, Miss McGregor; I'm not impressed."

Shasta's heart sank, but she remained silent. Why had Morgan led her to believe that the job was already hers?

"First you come a day early and now half an hour late. You've obviously taken very little time with your appearance, and I'll tell you the truth, if I didn't just have an employee quit on me, I'd probably be seeing you to the door."

Shasta nodded. What else could she do?

In truth, Kyle's estimation of her rose slightly when she didn't start to babble or try to offer excuses. He stared at her for a moment longer, thinking she was too young to be working for anyone, and then dropped his eyes to her resume. He read in silence until he got to her age.

"Is this correct? It says you're 32." He said the number with such disbelief that Shasta blushed.

"Yes, sir," she managed, all the while thinking that staying in Australia and facing the happily married Frank and DeeDee would have been preferable to this.

Kyle's cobalt blue eyes studied her from under slightly bushy brows. More silence followed as Kyle's eyes dropped to the papers and skimmed the sheets, not really reading the dates until another number jumped out at him.

"It says here that you've worked on a sheep ranch for 11 years."

"Yes sir."

"In the office?"

Shasta blinked and said softly, "No, sir. I'm sorry, but I don't know a thing about office work. Morgan said you needed a jackeroo."

"A what?" It was Kyle's turn to blink.

"Oh, uhm, a jackeroo, a ranch hand."

Kyle nodded slowly. Outside of a brief conversation a few weeks ago, it had been years since he'd talked to Morgan Clark, and he'd completely forgotten the little differences in their speech. He had to say one thing concerning Miss Shasta McGregor—that accent of hers was real easy on the ears.

"Why this ranch?"

"I beg your pardon?" Shasta was not prepared for the change in subject.

"What brings you to Harrington?"

"Oh, well," she stumbled slightly, her face paling some. "I was talking with Morgan, and he said you hired extra help in the summer. I thought I might enjoy the change."

Kyle could tell that there was more to this than what she'd just revealed and could only pray that this young woman was not in trouble with the law or in some other hairy situation. He did not take note of the fact that she had only just arrived in the United States before reading on.

"It says here that you rope and train."

"Yes, sir."

Again the eyes studied her; Shasta knew she was being weighed. "I'll give you a try, Miss McGregor. When can you start?"

Shasta took a deep breath. The last days were beginning to tell on her, and she knew she had to be honest.

"It's tempting to tell you that I can start right now, but in truth I need some rest. I didn't have breakfast, and my night was rough. If I could have some food and a place to bunk down, I can give you 100 percent of myself in the morning, or even later on this afternoon, but right now I wouldn't be much use to anyone."

Again Kyle's opinion of her rose. The ranch was in a rather remote area, and he could well guess in what type of place she must have stayed.

"All right," he said and rose. "I'll have Jean show you to your cabin and then the kitchen. I'll expect you on the job tomorrow morning at seven sharp."

"Thank you, Mr. Harrington."

He nodded, showed her to the door, told Jean what he needed, and disappeared back inside.

"Here," Jean offered immediately. "Let me carry your bag. You look all in."

"It was a long night," Shasta admitted as she lifted her saddle.

"Well, we'll get you all set in no time. I have some papers for you to fill out, but they can wait."

Her kindness was like a balm, and in little time Shasta had been shown her cabin and then taken to the kitchen for some food. Marcy, the camp cook, seemed to sense that she was too weary to converse and was silent while Shasta inhaled a plateful of food. She then made her way back to the cabin, ignoring the bathroom with its pristine shower stall, and collapsed onto her bed.

❧ ❧ ❧

"Okay, we've got strays to round up," Brian said to the group the afternoon of the next day. "Cal and Bennett can ride together, and Peter and Lloyd can go as a team. You'll ride with me, Shasta, and Lex, you can go with Scott."

"I thought Kyle wanted to go with us." This came from Scott, who was a regular at the ranch.

"Oh." Brian had not been aware of this. "I'll check with him."

"Did you want Shasta to go with us?" Lex asked a little too eagerly, and Brian worked at hiding a smile. Like Shasta and some of the others, Lex was there for the tourist season.

"No," he said kindly, "she can ride with me."

Scott was married, and Brian was engaged, but they understood Lex's interest in their new hand and exchanged smiles as only longtime friends could do. Lex, young and very single, missed the exchange, and Shasta, the object of nearly all the male eyes in the group, was working on a stirrup and missed the whole thing.

When Lex, Scott, and the others moved away, Brian turned to the newest member of Harrington Cattle Company.

"I've got to run to the office, Shasta. I'll be right back."

"All right," she replied, only glancing at him before going back to the work in her hands.

Brian left his horse at the fence and covered the ground with long strides. The door was open to Kyle's office, so he stepped right in.

"We're headed out for strays. Scotty mentioned that you wanted to go."

"Yes, I do," Kyle told him, feeling a need to be away from his desk. "Is it just the two of us?"

"No, we've got Shasta. I sent Lex with Scotty. I think he'll do better if Shasta is not around."

Kyle looked at him for a moment. "Like that, is it?"

Brian nodded. "Not that she's encouraged it," he was swift to add, "but he seems rather taken, as do some of the others."

Kyle's brows rose. "To each his own."

As the older man reached for his hat, Brian frowned at him in puzzlement but didn't speak. What in the world could he object to in Shasta's looks? Ah, well, it was not his place to question.

"Let's go," Kyle said.

The men, alike in height if not in build, walked side by side to the horses. Shasta had just swung onto her mount, Daisy, and didn't notice their approach, or she would have seen the check in Kyle's stride when he spotted her.

Kyle had not known what to expect where Shasta McGregor was concerned, but even before he saw her face, he could tell there was a change. The fatigue was gone—she had literally been drooping in the office chair the day before—and he could also tell in an instant that she'd spent many hours in a saddle. When she finally turned to face him, he was in for more of a surprise.

Makeup! Who in the world would wear makeup to work on a ranch? he asked himself, his brow drawn into a frown as he remembered that JoAnn had. Kyle was not happy with this thought.

Shasta, who didn't own makeup of any type, watched the emotions chase across her employer's face and experienced another feeling of dread. She'd eaten with the other hands that morning and done the chores given to her by Brian, but she hadn't given any thought to the reality that she was on trial. Now that fact became glaringly real.

It would be many weeks before Shasta knew what was in Kyle's heart. He was already pleased to see that she seemed to know her way around a ranch, but if she was husband hunting, he thought to himself, she had come to the wrong place.

❧ ❧ ❧

Two more days passed, and Shasta worked hard. It was not like her to ever sluff off. She was enjoying the work, and as she told Kyle, giving it her all. She hadn't seen that much of him, but somehow thought he might be pleased with her performance. This feeling lasted until Marcy cut her hand while working in the kitchen.

"Is it bad?" Brian asked, a few others, including Shasta, at his side.

"Yes," Kyle told him, his face concerned. "I'm taking her to the hospital. You're on your own for supper tonight."

Kyle turned away, but Shasta, not having understood what he meant, went after him.

"Kyle," she began, having been told the first day that they operated on a first-name basis. "What about supper? Would you like me to fix something?"

"The last thing I need is for you to be messing around the kitchen," he told her unkindly. "Like I said, you're on your own."

Shasta wasn't particularly hurt—she knew he was worried for Marcy—but she was confused. It was a relief to turn and find Brian standing right behind her.

"What does he mean when he says we're on our own?"

"For supper," Brian said and saw that it was still not clear to her. "In other words, we have to find our own supper."

Shasta looked surprised; she'd never heard of such a thing. Seeing her look, Brian hastened to explain.

"There are vending machines here at the rear of the kitchen, but there's also a snack bar at the hotel. None of us likes to dress up for the dining room, but you might like it."

"I'm sorry, Brian," Shasta said, her hands raised in defeat. "I've still no idea what you're talking about."

Brian kindly interpreted. "The guests arriving in a few days don't stay here at the ranch. They're guests of the Meadowland Hotel. They come by appointment to the ranch and are delivered by a van."

"Is the hotel a huge white structure to the east?"

"Yes," Brian smiled. "That's the one. Marcy keeps the vending machines stocked with sandwiches and fruit for the hands as well as the guests. So tonight with Marcy gone, we can use the machines, go up to the hotel, or even drive into town."

"I see," she smiled at him. "Thank you for explaining."

"What will you do?"

The question stumped her for a moment, and she scrambled for an answer.

"I haven't decided," she managed at last and was thankful Brian didn't press her. She wasn't sure why she felt ashamed, but the thought of telling him that she had no American currency was rather embarrassing to her.

"Well, I'll probably go to the snack bar," he said as he turned away. "If you want a ride, just let me know."

"Thank you, Brian."

They went their separate ways then, Shasta to her cabin and Brian to let the others know. Thankful she was rooming alone, Shasta sat on the edge of her bed for a moment and thought about her life in the last week. It seemed impossible that less than a week ago she'd been in the safe comfort of Burbarra.

"If I were to look at just the circumstances, Lord, I would say this has all been a mistake. I feel stranded and more lonely than I've ever been in my life. This is worse than when my folks died or when Frank broke off our engagement."

Thinking of Frank and saying his name out loud when she was finally private enough to give in to her emotions proved too much for Shasta. Tears filled her eyes, and she didn't even try to stem them. They poured down her face, and Shasta's breathing became ragged. Frank's rejection still hurt so much. He had said that he loved her and that he wanted her to be his forever, but she didn't hold a candle to DeeDee. Frank never actually said this, but it was all too clear.

Suddenly Shasta was very glad that she didn't have to face anyone for supper. She knew she would be hungry by breakfast, but for the time being, supper or no supper, Shasta was glad to have a reason to stay right where she was for the rest of the evening.

❧ ❧ ❧

It wasn't very late, not quite nine o'clock, but Shasta's lights were out. Kyle hesitated to do it, but he knew he had to knock. As his knuckles wrapped on the door, he wondered what he would do if she was out, but a light came on before he could go anywhere with the thought. A moment later, the door opened a crack.

"Who is it?"

"I'm sorry, Shasta," Kyle began. "I hate to disturb you, but I need to speak with you."

"All right." She sounded only slightly sleepy. "I'll be out in a shake."

She shut the door and let herself almost silently outside in less than five minutes. Kyle was some yards away, and as Shasta moved to join him, he saw that she'd donned pants, shirt, and boots. He felt bad that he'd disturbed her, but he didn't know what else to do.

"Is Marcy all right?" Shasta asked before Kyle could say a word.

"Yes, but the doctor says she needs to rest for a few days, and that's the reason I've come. First of all I need to apologize for the way I treated you when I left this afternoon. I have no excuse, and I'm truly sorry."

"I appreciate that," Shasta told him, "but I think I understand. Is there anything I can do to help?"

"As a matter of fact you can. Do you really know how to cook, or were you only trying to help out for tonight?"

"Well," Shasta said modestly but with a slight smile in her voice. "I've never cooked for more than 50, but I'll do my best if there are more."

Kyle smiled in her presence for the first time, and Shasta was amazed at the way it transformed his face. She didn't think he could be any more than ten years older than she was, but that smile made him look years younger. And Kyle kept right on smiling. He was swiftly coming to think that Shasta was an angel in blue jeans and dusty boots. Shasta finally smiled in return.

"It will just be for the 15 of us," Kyle told her, "and the food needs to be on the tables by 6:30 tomorrow morning."

"All right. Did you want me to fix anything in particular?"

"No. Cook whatever suits you, just as long as there's plenty and it's filling."

Shasta nodded. "I'm glad Marcy will be all right."

"Yes. She's supposed to lie low, but I doubt if that will last longer than a day. I'll have to let you know."

"That's fine."

"Are you certain?" he asked, and Shasta frowned at him. "I mean," he continued, his voice now very light, "you did hire on as a jackeroo."

"No worries," Shasta said, smiling, and Kyle grinned in return. There was no one else around, and the temperature had dropped with the sun.

"If that's all, I'll turn in now," Shasta said softly.

"Sure," Kyle agreed, his voice just as hushed. "Goodnight, Shasta, and thank you."

"You're welcome. Goodnight."

Kyle turned to watch her, telling himself he wanted to be sure she got back inside safely, but at the same time wondering why he was so sorry to see her go at all.

🌹 🌹 🌹

Kyle watched Shasta wipe sweat from her upper lip for the third time and wondered how in the world he could have mistaken her complexion for makeup. Up close he could see that she had skin like a perfectly made-up model.

He'd come in earlier to find her cutting onions and green peppers to go with the potatoes she was frying and asked if he could give a hand. She hadn't started the coffee, so he did that and now watched her turning pancakes with ease.

"Did you cook for Morgan?"

"Off and on. Peg took care of it most of the time, but over the years you pick up things."

"Well, I certainly appreciate your filling in."

Shasta smiled but did not answer, and a few moments later the others arrived. She put the food on the table, and sitting down, ate with the other hands, graciously accepting everyone's praise over the meal. She met Clare Sumner, Jean's sister-in-law, when she arrived to clean and cook until Marcy returned and finally went out with the others to work the range. It looked like it was going to be a long day.

❧ ❧ ❧

"You didn't tell me she was pretty," Clare spoke with familiar ease, her arms elbow deep in suds. She'd known Kyle since he was a little boy.

"Who?" Kyle pretended not to know.

"Shasta."

Kyle didn't speak for a moment, his mind on the woman who'd cooked that morning.

"She's a good worker," he finally said, his eyes on some distant spot.

Clare decided not to comment, and a moment later Kyle seemed to shake himself.

"I need to get going. Will you be all right?"

"Yes. How many for lunch?"

"About 20."

"All right. I'll have it ready."

Kyle took his leave then, his heart thoughtful as he thanked God for Clare's willingness to fill in. He also prayed on Marcy's behalf. He knew that the doctors would keep a close watch for infection, but he also knew that she would be chafing to be back in action soon. Moving his mind toward matters of the day, he walked toward the barn.

❧ ❧ ❧

You didn't tell me she was pretty. Clare's comment rang in Kyle's ears a few hours later as he watched Shasta in action and thought how true it was.

Shasta was pretty. She was also bright, fun, positive, encouraging, experienced, and hardworking, but she was not, as he'd originally believed, looking for a man.

In fact, Shasta McGregor was so unaware of the male attention she often received that she fascinated Kyle. Lex could barely keep his eyes off of her, and Bennett and Peter openly flirted with her on a regular basis. However, anytime the subject ranged to the personal, Shasta would simply smile and not reply. She didn't even acknowledge comments on the way she looked.

He had heard the men tell her that she was beautiful, that her hair was like a streak of sunshine down her back, and that her eyes were the largest and deepest brown they'd ever seen. All of which were offered in sincerity, but Shasta always looked slightly indulgent over these remarks, or at the very least, openly skeptical.

Kyle had never known anyone like her. He was going to be 45 on his next birthday, and for the first time in his life wondered whether they might not have become close, married even, if he'd met Shasta sooner. He knew it was too late now; he was too old to start such a life and change all of his ways, but even having the thought surprised him.

He mentally shook his head. The guests would be arriving even before they were ready, and he had no time for such contemplation. Determined to put his thoughts where they belonged, Kyle went back to work.

🌹 🌹 🌹

The day before the first guests were due, Marcy, who had come back to work in fine form, announced that she would be going into town after lunch to buy supplies. In need of some very personal items, Shasta debated what to do. She had yet to see a paycheck from the Harrington Cattle Company, and since she hadn't really become close to anyone at the ranch, she hesitated to ask anyone for money.

Kyle had been especially kind in the last few days, and after some thought, Shasta realized that she should go to him. He was in his office, and when he looked rather pleased to see her, Shasta felt emboldened.

"Kyle," she began. "Marcy is going into town this afternoon, and I wondered if you could spare me for a few hours?"

"Sure. The guests arrive tomorrow, and I won't be able to let you go much after that."

"Great, I'll plan on it," Shasta said but made no move to leave.

Coming to enjoy her company immensely, Kyle would have relished talking some more, but he had work to do.

"Was there anything else?"

Shasta cleared her throat and looked at her boots. "I'm afraid I'm a bit short of money." She watched him frown. "I can give it right back to you on payday—" she hastened to add, but the phone rang.

Kyle picked it up, and Shasta saw immediately that he needed privacy. She moved toward the door, glancing back before exiting, but Kyle didn't even notice her. With a prayer for wisdom she went outside to work.

Hours later Scott was in the office with Kyle. The phone call that morning had been important, and the news had effectively wiped all other thoughts from his mind.

"Okay, I think that wraps it up. Go right now and tell Marcy that—"

"Marcy went into town," Scott reminded him.

"Oh, that's right." Some of Kyle's memory was now returning. "Shasta was going with her."

"Shasta didn't go."

"She didn't?"

"No," Scott told him, giving little thought to it. "She rode out with Lex and Cal. See you later. I'll leave a note for Marcy."

"All right. Thanks, Scotty."

The phone rang, much as it had been doing all day, and it was still another two hours before Kyle saw Shasta. He had not searched her out but saw her across the dining room. They didn't speak then, but when the meal was over he caught up with her as she headed toward her cabin.

"I'm sorry about this morning, Shasta. Did you have Marcy get your things for you?"

"Well, no," Shasta said a bit uncomfortably, thinking that it never occurred to her to go directly to Marcy.

"Oh, well," Kyle said, not noticing her discomfort. "She goes in fairly often. I'm certain she'll help you out if you'll let her know."

"Sure." Shasta smiled and started away, but once again his voice turned her.

"I've just remembered that you said you needed money."

Shasta turned back but didn't say anything. Earlier she'd had the nerve to ask, but right now it felt humiliating. She found it easier to stay silent, but Kyle spoke up.

"I'd completely forgotten." He was reaching for his wallet, but without a ride to town Shasta wasn't sure it would do her much good. "Will this be enough?"

"Yes," Shasta answered without even looking at the bills. "Thank you." She would have turned away, but Kyle asked conversationally,

"How did you manage to run out of money?"

"It was foolish of me," Shasta admitted. "But I was so tired when I landed that I didn't even think to have my bills changed over."

Shasta stuffed the money into the front pocket of her jeans, and Kyle studied her. She was once again on the verge of turning away when Kyle asked, "What do you mean, 'when you landed?'"

"When I got into the airport at San Francisco. Morgan said I could change money there, but I completely forgot."

Shasta suddenly found her arm in Kyle's large hand, and he was leading her to some lawn chairs at the side of the ranch house. No one was about, and Shasta was glad since it looked like Kyle was going to lay into her. She didn't know what she'd done, but he looked thunderstruck.

"Shasta," he began after he'd nearly pushed her into a chair. "Haven't you been living in America for a while?"

"No."

"When did you arrive?"

"Let's see," she thought to get it right. "It was the day before my interview."

Kyle swallowed. "How did you get up here?"

"On the bus."

"With what?"

Shasta stared at him a moment. "Oh! Peg had some American currency, and it turned out to be just enough."

"So you flew from Sydney—"

"No, Brisbane."

"All right. You flew out of Brisbane, landed at SFO, and then got on a bus and came right up here?"

"Yes."

"But I didn't interview you until the next day."

"Right."

"Shasta," Kyle continued, beginning to feel slightly horrified, "where did you go that night?"

"Back up the road," Shasta said simply. "There was a large outcropping of rock. I'm sure I was on private land, but no one disturbed me."

"You slept outside on the ground?" He was looking so alarmed that she tried to reassure him.

"It's not the first time."

"That's beside the point. What did you do for food?"

"Well, you fed me after the interview."

He took a moment to think about this. "What about the other night, when Marcy cut herself?"

Shasta grinned. "I wasn't all that hungry."

"Goodnight, Nellie," Kyle muttered under his breath, dipping his head to rub the back of his neck.

"I beg your pardon?"

"No, Shasta," he said softly as he raised his eyes to hers, "I beg *yours*. I had no idea. I thought Morgan said that you were an Aussie living here in the states. I never dreamed you'd only just arrived. You must have wondered what kind of man I was to treat you in such a way."

"No," Shasta told him with a shake of her head. "Some of it was my fault. I could have asked for help."

Kyle didn't agree but remained silent. He had not been at all kind to her when she'd come, and as he thought back, he'd have been more surprised if she *had* asked for aid. His mind moved on to everything she'd revealed. Some of the people who roamed the area were not to be trusted, and he couldn't sanction the thought of her sleeping outside.

"I get the feeling that you're used to doing things on your own, Shasta, but it's not that safe around here."

"Well, I've my cabin now; I won't need the rocks." Her voice was light, but Kyle didn't smile.

"But you do need to get to town?"

"Well," Shasta replied, knowing this might be her last chance. "I do need some things. If I recall, it's a pretty fair walk."

"I'll take you," he immediately answered and stood. With a relieved prayer of thanks, Shasta followed suit. "Let me tell Jean where I'll be." Walking toward the office Kyle asked, "What did you need?"

They were walking side by side, and when Shasta didn't answer, Kyle looked down to see her face lit up like a stoplight. He was old enough and wise enough to see that he'd blundered, and as Shasta moved to his truck, he knew he would need to refrain from making further comment or inquiries.

❧ ❧ ❧

"I think ice cream sounds good. Are you game?"

Shasta smiled. "It does sound good, but I'm the one who had to borrow money just a few hours ago, so I—"

"If that's all that's stopping you, I'll take that as a yes."

Shasta had nothing else to say to this and sat quietly while Kyle pulled up before a small ice cream parlor. They were reaching for their door handles when Kyle said, "Were you able to get all you needed?"

Shasta blushed again, but Kyle wanted an answer.

"Shasta, if you say yes when you mean no, I'll fire you."

It was just what she needed, and with laughter in her voice she said, "I have everything I need, *providing* I will eventually get a paycheck."

"Thursday."

"Great."

The remainder of the evening was spent in companionable fellowship, but the conversation never ranged to the personal. Once Shasta arrived back at her cabin, she put her things away and prepared for bed, but her mind was still on her boss. He was nothing like she had previously believed, and she was still getting used to her new impression. He was still strong on her mind when she finally climbed into bed and dropped off to sleep.

❧ ❧ ❧

"This is not the horse I wanted!" An angry voice split the air, and Shasta thought the ache in her head would split her skull as well. It was already the fifth week of working with the hotel patrons, and for some reason Shasta couldn't please anyone on this particular day. This certainly accounted for the headache, but it also didn't help that she was furious with her boss. The girl she'd been teaching to ride that morning had been hurt, and Kyle had blamed Shasta. He had come on the scene without knowing the facts and passed immediate judgment. Shasta had stood silently and taken the rebuke, but she was furious inside.

That night at supper she barely touched her food, and just as soon as she was able, she moved back to the stables and saddled a mount. She was still working on the cinch when she heard footsteps and then Kyle's voice behind her.

"I'm really disappointed, Shasta."

The small blonde only turned and stared at him.

"You don't strike me as the type to pout."

"I'm not pouting," Shasta said, going back to the saddle. "I just don't care to be anywhere near you right now."

If Shasta had been looking behind her, she'd have seen Kyle's brows fly upward. He wasn't used to this kind of bluntness.

"Where are you going?"

Shasta answered from the saddle. "For a ride."

Kyle was not satisfied, but he wasn't going to baby her.

"Are we ever going to talk about this?"

"Yes. When I'm calm enough to say what needs to be said."

"And what exactly needs to be said, Shasta?" His voice demanded an answer.

"Well, for starters you made a judgment without knowing all the facts," Shasta told him, her voice angry. "Did you know she was 14?"

"*Fourteen?*"

"That's right. She lied to you."

"You had no business taking a 14-year-old out like that!" He was at her again.

"I didn't know until we'd ridden out to the middle of nowhere and she fell on her head! *You've* got no business taking someone's word and not their ID."

With that Shasta wheeled her horse around and took off. Kyle watched her for long minutes. She was an excellent rider, he had to give her that. He thought he'd been more than justified in raking her over the coals for risking the safety of a client, but as she stated, he hadn't known all the facts.

Taking note of the exact direction Shasta was headed, Kyle moved to the stall that housed his horse. Inside of ten minutes he was mounted up and riding out. His destination: wherever he would find Shasta McGregor.

❧ ❧ ❧

Shasta rode hard for the next half an hour, not in fury, but with a need to run. She gave the horse its head and sat back for the enjoyment. When her mount finally slowed to a halt, Shasta let her take her ease. In fact, she had dismounted and was walking alongside of Daisy, the reins hanging from her hand, when Kyle caught up to her. He dismounted as well, and for a time they walked in companionable silence.

"The biggest disappointment," Shasta suddenly said, "is that I thought you were better than that."

"Meaning?"

"Meaning, I could see that girl was underage from ten yards away. Surely girls have tried that before and you haven't fallen for it."

She had him there. Why hadn't he seen how young she was?

"That's true," he finally commented, but Shasta was just warming up and gave him no quarter.

"And you tell me the customer is always right. Is that what I'm to say on the witness stand when someone sues the socks off of you? *The customer is right, judge. I mean, she lied to us about her age and ability, but she got hurt, so no matter what, you should still award her the property deed to the Harrington Cattle Company.*"

Kyle's shoulders shook with silent laughter, and Shasta gave him a sidelong glance.

"Honestly, Kyle, what was I supposed to do?"

He shook his head. "Right now I don't know. All I heard was that when you had Miss Presley out on the hardest trail, she was injured."

"She insisted on that trail," Shasta told him. "She told me she'd been riding since she was a child, not to mention the fact that she smiled and flashed those eyes at you, and you said I should take her wherever she wanted to go. Again I ask you, what was I supposed to do?"

Kyle stopped, and Shasta followed suit. "If you could see she was that young, why did you take her up onto Bracken Ridge? I'd have thought that would have been enough to cause you to defy me."

Shasta opened her mouth and closed it. A spark of humor lit Kyle's eyes even as his brows rose upward.

"It looks like we both owe each other an apology," Kyle said softly.

Shasta put her hand out. "Here's mine."

Kyle took her hand in his larger one and held it for a moment. "God was smiling on the Harrington Cattle Company the day He sent you our way, Shasta McGregor."

Shasta smiled. "I rather like it here myself."

They mounted up again and continued their ride. They talked off and on, but most of the time was spent in amicable silence. The ranch was thousands of acres large, and both felt they would be content to ride for hours. However, the setting sun drove them back toward the ranch, and they had to settle for just one. Everything was quiet by the time they arrived, and again they fell mute as if in reverence for the silent surroundings.

"I'll see you in the morning, Shasta," Kyle told her and watched as she lifted a hand and started toward her cabin.

Kyle had planned to get some things done after supper, but since he'd gone out, he was now forced to move toward his office. He was hoping not to be disturbed, but the phone rang.

"That you, Kyle?"

"Morgan! How are you?"

"I'm fine. How about yourself?"

"Busy, but doing well. Shasta's a real help."

"How is she?"

"She's doing great. Hasn't she been in touch at all?"

"She has, but since I can't see her face, I'm not completely satisfied. And Peg worries from time to time."

"I think she's doing well."

"Has she made some friends?"

"Definitely. All the workers like her."

A silence fell on the other end, and Kyle asked, "Are you worried about something, Morgan?"

"Not really, but has she, oh, you know, shared anything with you, Kyle?" Morgan's voice was hesitant.

"About her personal life? Not really. She told me one day that her parents have been dead for years, but no one really knows why she left Australia."

Kyle listened to Morgan sigh on the other end.

"If you want to share, Morgan, you know I'll be discreet."

Again the sigh. "Shasta was to be married this Saturday, but he broke it off. It sounds like she's doing well, but I just need someone there to keep an eye on her."

"You can count on me; you know that."

"Thanks, Kyle. Peg just sent a letter off that should arrive before the twenty-ninth, but if it doesn't, I just want her to know someone cares."

"I'll keep an eye on her. She tends to keep to herself to a certain extent, but that might be self-preservation, since some of the men are falling over themselves to be noticed."

Morgan's laugh cracked over the line. "Peg told her that would happen, but she didn't believe her."

"I can believe that. She hardly notices them."

"Well, that's too bad. I'd love to have her come back to us, but that's being selfish. If she found someone there who would cherish her, we'd be delighted."

"It's probably too soon," Kyle commented, and Morgan couldn't help but agree. They talked a little longer and then said their goodbyes.

Kyle sat back in his chair. He didn't feel like working at his desk any longer. Years ago Kyle had fallen in love with a woman who considered him only a friend. It had not jaded him for life, but the pain had been intense for years after. Right now his heart clenched as he envisioned Shasta's face in his mind. It was still paining him the next morning when he sought Shasta out in the barn. He stood on the other side of the horse she was saddling, his height making it easy to see her over the top of the horse's back.

"Are you free for dinner on Saturday night?"

Shasta froze in her boots and looked up at him. With a single knuckle she pushed the brim of her hat higher and continued to stare.

"Dinner?"

"Yes, in Jenner, just the two of us."

Shasta blinked at him and then smiled. "I would like that, especially if I can wear a dress."

Kyle's rugged features broke into a return smile. "In that case I'll have on a suit and tie."

Shasta went back to work then, her heart light. No thoughts of romance entered her sensible head, but an evening out with Kyle Harrington and a chance to dress up a little was something to anticipate. It made the week seem very short indeed.

❧ ❧ ❧

Shasta woke up on Saturday morning and stared into space. How had the time moved so swiftly? Today she was supposed to become Mrs. Frank Iverson. Shasta rolled over in bed and buried her face in her pillow. Why in the world had she agreed to go out tonight? Right now all she wanted was to be alone.

Such thoughts tortured Shasta as she readied for the day's work and made her too late to even eat breakfast. Kyle was one of the first persons she saw, and he knew instantly that she was upset. Thanking God that he knew the reason, he decided to keep her as busy as possible. Indeed, she didn't have a moment to herself until after four o'clock, at which time Kyle approached her.

"I'd like to leave here about 5:30, Shasta, so you can take off any time."

"All right. Are you sure you still want to go?"

Kyle's brows rose.

"I mean," Shasta stumbled, "it's been a long day, and I thought you might be tired."

Again Kyle only stared at her before saying, "Five-thirty, Shasta."

The petite blonde went to her cabin then, but her heart was in a quandary. She was well on her way to wholeness after Frank's rejection, but unlike the first of the week, a date with Kyle now seemed too personal and romantic.

"Well, there's no help for it at this point," she told the cabin at large. "He's coming, and you still smell like a horse."

With that she readied for a shower and shampoo. She didn't linger for fear of being late and only partially dried her hair. For the first time since arriving, she didn't put it back in a braid; a braid never worked well when her hair was wet. She drew the sides back with combs and let the back hang free. She looked lovely when Kyle answered the door, but there was pain behind her eyes. Kyle didn't miss a thing, but he only commented to the positive, telling her she looked very nice.

Shasta thanked him demurely and was surprised when he led her to a beautiful dark gray sports car. She hadn't known he owned such a vehicle.

"You thought we were going in the truck," Kyle laughed when he was behind the wheel.

Shasta smiled a little. "I guess I did. I wouldn't have minded."

Kyle started the car then, and they made the drive in silence. The restaurant was set on a clifftop that overlooked the sea, and Kyle had asked for a table by the window. Shasta took note of the fact that he was known by nearly everyone they passed, and his greeting to all of them was friendly.

"What are you hungry for?"

"I don't know. It all looks so good."

"It's not Friday, but the fish is great; so is the beef."

"Harrington beef?" Shasta asked.

"What else?" Kyle said with a grin.

A few minutes later they ordered, Shasta going with a steak and Kyle opting for chicken. Their waiter had just brought them an appetizer when Kyle asked Shasta how she liked the ranch.

"It's beautiful, Kyle. It's a summer I'll never forget."

"But you look forward to going home?"

Shasta stared down at the beach as the waves crashed endlessly against the sand.

"I don't know," she finally admitted. "In some ways I wish it was more than just summer work, and in others I miss Burbarra so much that I ache."

Kyle didn't comment. Shasta finally looked at him.

"It was a hard day today."

"Do you want to talk about it?"

Shasta hesitated, and Kyle cut back in.

"Don't even answer that, Shasta, if it's going to ruin your evening."

"No, it's all right, Kyle. I haven't talked with anyone, and I think it might be nice, but that's not the way you want to spend your evening."

Kyle shook his head slightly. "Why was it a hard day?"

It was all Shasta needed.

"I was to be married today. At eleven o'clock this morning I was going to marry Frank Iverson."

"What happened?"

"DeeDee Wharton happened. They had dated years before I met him, and after we'd become engaged, she returned to Brisbane and Frank fell back in love with her. I'm only glad it didn't happen later, you know, after we'd said our vows."

Kyle nodded.

"And that's why you left Australia?"

"Yes. I saw Frank and DeeDee every week, and Morgan told me to go. I didn't want to at first, but I think it's been very therapeutic. Like I said, I'm torn about going back."

"You might not be in another six weeks. Well, more like eight with roundup."

Shasta nodded, and a moment later their salads arrived. The food was marvelous, and the conversation never waned. Shasta learned that Kyle was nearly 45 and the oldest in his family. Shasta elaborated on her parents' deaths, and they both shared memories of their childhoods and the way they had come to Christ at a young age. Kyle was a wonderful dinner companion, and Shasta was very thankful that she hadn't talked herself out of going.

They were still talking when they arrived back at the ranch, and Kyle asked Shasta in for coffee. The ranch house was gorgeous: warm and homey and beautifully decorated. He told Shasta he'd had it all professionally done, but she was both pleased and amazed to find that Kyle himself had made the cake she was eating. He brewed a mean cup of coffee as well, and it was after eleven when she said she had better turn in or she'd never be able to get going for church.

Kyle walked her back to her cabin, and once at the door asked, "If I asked you out again, Miss McGregor, would you go?"

"Well now," Shasta told him. "It depends on the reason. Would you be asking me because you feel sorry about what I've told you or because you enjoyed my company?"

"I am sorry for your hurt, Shasta," Kyle told her sincerely, "but if I asked you out again, it would be for the sole reason that I find you delightful to talk with."

Shasta smiled. "In that case, I hope you ask."

Kyle smiled as well and then thanked her.

"For what?" Shasta had no idea.

"For wearing your hair in a braid when we work. If you didn't, we wouldn't get a thing done."

They both said goodnight on Shasta's light laughter.

❧ ❧ ❧

The first date was the start of a pattern. Shasta and Kyle went to dinner every Saturday night. Most nights they dressed more casually, but each evening was long, with good food and hours of talk. An odd thing was happening in Shasta's heart. Frank Iverson was receding more and more every week into the back of her mind, but her thoughts and feelings for Kyle did not involve romance or marriage. It was just utterly delightful to have a male friend, one who cared for her and with whom it was easy to talk. Thoughts of returning to Australia never entered her head, so she was never forced to ask herself how she would leave him or the ranch.

Kyle, on the other hand, was in a totally different camp. By roundup he realized that he had fallen very much in love with Shasta McGregor. He didn't think she was still pining for her Australian, but like the other woman from years ago, it would seem that she saw him as more of a friend than anything else. He didn't know if God had something more for him, but he prayed that if He did, it would reveal itself some-time during the two-week roundup.

A stir of excitement ran among the hands after the appointments with the hotel guests ended. Marcy and her husband, Leroy, always went on roundup, but this year Shasta would need the wagon as well, so Leroy would stay home, and Shasta would bunk with Marcy. At times an all-male camp was interesting for Shasta, but since she'd worked with the lot of them for weeks, she blended right in. Marcy was old enough to be a mother and maybe grandmother to all of them, so she thought little of their bare chests and trips into the bushes.

Peter was still doing his level best to get a date with her, but Shasta could not be swayed. She merely smiled without answering and ofttimes debated if she should tell the 19-year-old that she was 13 years his senior. On the second night Kyle came to her rescue. It looked as if Peter was going to pursue her the entire drive, but after supper, with all the other hands in attendance, Kyle asked Shasta to join him for a walk. Quite certain they were being watched, he even picked up her hand as they wandered away.

"Thanks," Shasta told him when they were out a ways.

"You're welcome," Kyle told her but kept her hand. It felt warm and comforting to Shasta, so she didn't pull away. They walked along for some time, neither feeling a need to talk, but Shasta was doing plenty of thinking. The time had crept upon her so suddenly. She was scheduled to leave in less than two weeks. What had happened to the summer?

She suddenly glanced down at the hand holding hers. How would she walk away from this man? While on their second date, weeks ago, Kyle had told Shasta that he felt he waited too long to marry. *I'm pretty settled in,* he'd said that night. *I assume that any woman who would have me would also want children, and I can't imagine starting a family at my age. I guess I'm thankful that God has made me content to be as I am.*

His words had not been a problem then, but now they chilled Shasta to the bone. As carefully as possible she let her hand slip from Kyle's. She glanced away from him in an attempt to seem casual, so she missed the longing in Kyle's eyes. They both began thought patterns that nearly echoed each other's, but were both all wrong.

It's time to build up a wall, Kyle, old boy. She's going to leave here, and it's going to kill you if you don't stop this longing.

Shasta's line of reasoning was no different. *He's had all summer to find his heart, but by his own admission, he's happy alone. Get your mind back in order, Shasta, or getting on the plane is going to tear you apart.*

The sun was dropping fast, bringing with it the cool night temperature. They turned back toward camp, both still silent, alone, and miserable with their thoughts.

❧   ❧   ❧

"Okay, Bennett," Kyle yelled as the cows surged forward. "Let's head home."

The driving force behind the Harrington Cattle Company followed more slowly, glad to be at the rear even though they were so near the ranch. The last two weeks had been some of the hardest of Kyle's life. Loving Shasta and yet trying to keep his distance had been almost more than he could take. It was late on Sunday, and her flight was scheduled for the next afternoon. In some ways he was relieved, since he would no longer need to pretend, but he knew that it was going to take more than a few days, possibly years, before he would forget.

His mind conjured up a sudden image of her calling and asking if he needed her the next summer. The thought alone caused his eyes to close in pain. *I'm too old to go through this, Lord. I've never dated around. I've never been the type to fall in and out of love with the changing of the seasons. It hurts too much.*

"Stampede!"

The shout rang out, and Kyle opened his eyes in a hurry. To the west and a quarter of a mile away, more than a hundred head of cattle were running hard away from the main body of the herd. Shouting to Brian and Shasta to take the rest in, Kyle reined his horse hard and followed Scott, Cal, and Bennett at a breakneck speed. His rifle was already drawn, and he was circling the runaways with experience born of years in the saddle.

The hands taking the herd in heard the gunshots and shouts as the strays were put in place, but they had ridden so hard and fast that they were nearly out of sight. At one point three shots went up in a row, and both Brian and Shasta stood in their stirrups to see. A second later the shots came again, and Brian, who still hadn't seen anything, began to shout.

"Ride for the ranch, Shasta! Call for an ambulance!"

She wheeled her horse and dug in her heels and a moment later she was flying toward the ranch that could easily be seen in the distance. Her only prayer, selfish as it was, was to beg God not to let it be Kyle.

❧ ❧ ❧

"How is he?" Shasta asked Kyle's surgeon as she and Brian met him in the hallway at the hospital.

"He's stable but still out. If it had only been the leg, I wouldn't have been too concerned, but he took a major blow to the head."

Shasta began to tremble. She didn't even feel Brian's arm come around her.

"I need to see him," she said, tears filling her eyes.

"He's still in recovery, but someone will come for you as soon as he's moved." The doctor touched her shoulder and moved away, and Shasta turned helplessly to the foreman.

"I never told him, Brian. I never told him how I felt."

"You'll get your chance, Shasta; it's all right. Kyle's as tough as they come. You just wait and see."

Brian looked up to see the others arriving: Leroy and Marcy, Jean and her husband, as well as most of the hands. They began a night-long vigil in the waiting room, and some of them were finally allowed to see a still-sleeping Kyle. Shasta felt better just standing next to him, but her need to talk with him was so great that all she could do was cry. Jean finally led her to her car and took her back to the ranch. She spoke words of comfort, but Shasta knew that what she needed most was to be alone and pray. Even after Jean walked her to her cabin, Shasta did not sleep but fell to her knees and asked God for comfort, mercy, and grace. She prayed the night away and then fell into an exhausted sleep that lasted until late in the day on Monday. She finally made it to the hospital on Monday evening, her heart calm. Not until she was alone with Kyle on Tuesday morning did he wake up and speak with her. Shasta had been sitting by his bed for the best part of 30 minutes when she saw that his eyes were open.

"What day is it?" he croaked.

"Tuesday."

He stared at her a long minute. Finally, "Your flight left yesterday. Why are you still here?"

Shasta shrugged helplessly, thinking he would know. "I'm not exactly sure myself," she finally managed.

Kyle's hand moved on the sheet, turning palm up, his fingers reaching. Shasta gently placed her hand within his grasp.

"If you can wait until I get out of this bed, I'll give you a reason."

Tears flooded Shasta's eyes and streamed down her face. Kyle reached and gently caught a drop on his finger. He then took her hand again and fell asleep as he held it. Shasta lay her forehead on the edge of the mattress and sobbed with relief and the love she'd held inside. She'd been so afraid of his rejection, and now she felt tired all over. When the nurse came to check on Kyle just five minutes later, they were both sound asleep.

❧ ❧ ❧

Shasta passed Marcy on the way into the ranch house a week and a half later. She hadn't seen much of Kyle in that time because she'd spent so much time working with Brian and Scott at the ranch. The summer help had gone home, and she felt the best place she could be was working and lightening any anxiety Kyle might have over the herd. He'd been home a few days, but with his leg in a cast up to his thigh, he was pretty immobile. He'd also been sleeping much of the time, but he'd sent someone to find her that afternoon.

"He's in the living room," Marcy told her, "and I can see by his face that he means business."

Shasta nodded, thanked her, and moved inside. She left her hat in the front hall and moved soft-footedly to the edge of the living room.

Kyle was sitting on one end of the sofa, his leg stretched out over the cushions. He had a perfect view of the door, and for a moment they just stared at each other.

"Come here, Shasta," he called in a soft, low voice.

Shasta came halfway across the room and stopped by a chair. Kyle's hand came up, and he motioned to her with one finger, but Shasta shook her head.

"I think I'd better stay here." She felt and sounded oddly nervous.

It was Kyle's turn to shake his head. "Come here, Shasta."

Shasta came a bit closer but eyed him warily. His look was intense as he held her eyes with his own. Again he motioned to her, and Shasta came to what she thought was a safe distance. She was wrong. Kyle's hand shot out and captured her wrist. A moment later she was sitting on the edge of the sofa, held close in Kyle's arms while he kissed her.

"What was that?" she gasped when he finally raised his head.

"A reason to stay. And if it isn't enough, maybe this will be." His face was still close, his voice hushed. "I love you, Shasta McGregor."

"Oh, Kyle," she breathed, and he kissed her again.

Kyle suddenly broke the kiss. "Do you want to be married here or in Australia?"

Shasta laughed. "I take it you're asking me to marry you?"

Kyle's smile was huge. "Well, it's either ask you or tell you."

Again Shasta laughed. "I thought you said you were happy alone."

Kyle laid his forehead against hers. "I've been praying for weeks that you'd forgotten all about that."

Shasta's eyes now took on a moment of pain. "I couldn't think of anything else. That was why I was leaving."

Kyle's huge hand cupped her cheek, and he kissed her again.

"I've waited a very long time for you, Shasta, and I didn't even know I was looking. I thought you wanted to return to Australia, or I'd have never let you go."

Shasta stared at him for a long time. He shifted her in his arms, and she remembered his cast.

"You're not really in shape to walk down the aisle right now, are you?"

"Six weeks."

Shasta's brows rose. "Is that what the doctor says?"

"He said eight, but if you'll marry me when this cast is off, I'll make it six."

Shasta smiled complacently.

"You didn't say where you wanted to be married."

The lovely petite blonde cocked her head to the side. "I think we should marry here and honeymoon in Australia. What do you think?"

"I think that there couldn't be a happier man on either continent."

With that, Shasta kissed him.

A Note from Lori: *I have no idea if anyone on the northern California coastline actually has roundup, but this story was so fun in my mind that I didn't care if I had the facts correct. Jenner, Bodega Bay, Goat Rock, Occidental, Schoolhouse Beach, and many more beaches and towns are places I love to visit. My father drove a propane truck for more than 27 years, and this was his route for much of that time. For that reason, along with the fact that my memories of these places are sweet, I needed to put a special couple like Kyle and Shasta on the coast where I spent so much time growing up.*